The Disappearance By The Amish River

Terri Downes

Published by Trellis Publishing, 2021.

THE DISAPPEARANCE BY THE AMISH RIVER

First edition. July 1, 2021.

Copyright © 2021 Terri Downes.

ISBN: 979-8224404544

Written by Terri Downes.

THE DISAPPEARANCE BY THE AMISH RIVER

Terri Downes

"Excuse me."

Hannah stopped in her tracks and glanced at the desk sergeant, half expecting him to ask her stop pacing, He had already been shooting her dirty looks for the past half hour.

"Detective Brenner can see you now."

Hannah followed the sergeant's gesture to the detective's desk, where she stood awkwardly for a few moments, waiting for the older woman to stop her typing.

"I've looked at the letter," said Detective Brenner, barely glancing up.

"And?" asked Hannah, though from the lack of urgency she could guess the answer.

"I understand why it might have made you worry," said the detective. "But there's nothing in here that warrants an investigation."

"But the writer – Adriane Smith – she says she's afraid something might happen to her." Hannah pointed at the tattered sheet of paper lying on the desk. "And she wrote the letter the day she disappeared, five years ago."

"I was curious as to how you worked that out," said Detective Brenner.

"I googled it," shrugged Hannah.

"And the reason the letter was in your possession in the first place?"

Now the detective was looking at Hannah directly. Hannah flushed under her scrutiny.

"I said. A friend called me. Adriane was staying at the house as a lodger when she disappeared, and my friend found the letter in her loft when she was clearing it out. It was in an old trunk with Adriane's things that were never collected."

"Why? Why call you, and not the police?"

"My friend thought she would be helping me," admitted Hannah. "I haven't had a big story in a while."

"Right. A story. Because you're a reporter."

The detective said the word *reporter* with distaste.

"I'm not after a headline," said Hannah, wishing she didn't sound so defensive.

"Aren't you? You bring me a letter that this missing woman supposedly wrote and never mailed, you don't even wait for us to look at the letter before you start spouting theories – "

"I was trying to explain why I thought it was important," said Hannah. "Adriane was clearly scared when she wrote the letter. She says she's discovered something troubling and she needs to get help."

"But she didn't get help," said the detective. "She wrote the letter, left it buried in her other belongings, and then skipped out on her landlady without paying her final rent check. That's all. If she needed help, she'd have called the police, not written a letter. This isn't the 1800s."

"She was writing to an Amish friend," said Hannah. "A woman she had been staying with that summer, while she was studying the river with her professor and some other PHD candidates. The woman wouldn't have had a phone. Maybe she saw Adriane before she disappeared?"

"Sure, the Amish always make a good news story," said the detective, rolling her eyes. "People always want to read about religious weirdos."

"I said that's not what I'm –"

"Look, you feel free to go knocking on doors in the depths of Amish country," said the detective, going back to her typing. "Call me if you trip over a body. Or maybe I'll catch the story when it breaks."

"I'd rather go back to covering the traffic than head into Amish country," muttered Hannah.

This earned a short laugh from the detective, but no further comment, and Hannah gave up the conversation. As she left the station, the desk sergeant beckoned her over.

"Don't be offended," he said. "We get a lot of local reporters in here trying to scrape for stories. She's at the end of her patience."

"I really do think something might have happened, though," said Hannah.

This, however, got nothing more than a sympathetic shrug.

It was perhaps her irritation at both the unsympathetic and the sympathetic responses, both of which had been equally infuriating, that led Hannah onto the highway and toward the turnoff for the "Amish country" she had been so determined to avoid.

She had not been anywhere near the area in fifteen years, and had sworn she never would again.

But if she was right...

Hannah had not reported on a big story in a long time. She knew her career should be advancing at a more rapid pace. She had never been as ambitious as her colleagues, relying on a gradual climb that provided steady work and good experience. But as she approached her thirties, she had begun to worry about whether she was where she should be.

And Madison finding that letter in her loft had seemed like fate.

Or something else, a small voice said in the back of her mind. She ignored the voice. She had had to face that fact that God had no particular plans for her a long while ago.

Even if it weren't fate, she would have to an idiot to let this go. It might be a big story. If her hunch was right, there might even be a killer who was still out there.

***

The letter that Adriane had written on the last day anyone remembered seeing her had been addressed to Mary Hill, at River Rush Farm.

On her way there, Hannah stopped at a diner to plan. She called around to reach members of the team Adriane had been working with that summer, five years ago. She asked why Adriane would have written to her old landlady a month after leaving the farm.

Most of the people Hannah spoke to directed her to call Daisy Henry, who had been the closest with Adriane.

"They became good friends over the summer," Adriane's old professor told Hannah. "Daisy was so upset when Adriane disappeared without saying goodbye."

Daisy claimed, however, that Adriane had been even better friends with her landlady, Mary.

"The rest of us were staying at the bed and breakfast for the summer," she said. "Adriane wanted to be closer to the research site at the river, so she got this little cottage at the end of a farmer's field. I guess the old woman must have been lonely, because they were always off having tea together or whatever."

Hannah supposed it made sense that Adriane would try to contact her friend, having left the farm just a few weeks before she wrote the letter.

Still, it was odd that someone so modern, headed into the world of academics, would make friends with her Amish landlady. Or rather that the landlady would have made friends with her.

As Hannah got out of the car, the scent of sun-warmed earth and grass lifted to greet her. She almost reeled back at the memories the smell brought with it.

Those long, hot days she had spent in the countryside, enjoying the silence. Looking forward to more. Her mother telling her that this would be their life, soon. Her mother laughing.

Hannah shook her head and faced the farmhouse. She could see someone moving inside, and braced herself for the conversation.

They probably wouldn't even talk to her, an outsider. She was wasting her time.

The door opened, and Hannah was taken aback to see a young man standing there. Or maybe he wasn't young. He couldn't have been older than she was, anyway.

"Hi, is Mary Hill here?" asked Hannah, wondering if she should show her press credentials. Would it matter?

"She passed away," replied the man, in the strange accent Hannah remembered associating with this area.

"Oh. Did you buy the farm after she died?"

"I inherited it," said the man. "I'm her son."

"I didn't know she had children," said Hannah in surprise. All of Adriane's old colleagues had said Mary lived alone. "I'm sorry for your loss," she added, wishing it did not sound like an afterthought.

She quickly launched into a short explanation of why she was here. The man listened quietly, not showing any reaction.

"Have you contacted the police?" he asked, after she was done.

"Yes, but you don't have to worry, they didn't take me seriously," sighed Hannah.

The man raised an eyebrow.

"I find that very worrying indeed. What if something happened to Adriane?"

"I thought you would want the police to stay away," said Hannah.

"Why would I want that?" said the man, frowning.

"They're outsiders," said Hannah.

The man looked at her for a moment with a serious expression, then stepped out of the house and closed the door behind him.

"If something happened to Adriane, we should help," he said. "Come on, I'll show you the cottage. No-one's stayed there since her."

On the walk across the fields, the man introduced himself as Peter. It seemed he had never met Adriane, as he had been staying with his uncle the summer she was at the farm.

"My mother told me all about her, though, and about the studies she was doing. My mother said Adriane wanted to record a new species

– moss I think it was, and it had something in it that could be used in medicines."

"And the local people didn't mind a load of scientists wandering around?"

"Why would we mind? They kept to themselves," said Peter. "My mother said they were very nice."

"But science and religion hardly mix," said Hannah.

Peter gave her a sideways glance.

"I take it you disapprove of religion."

Hannah tensed herself, ready for an argument.

"I think any way of life that values rules over people isn't worth the effort."

Peter glanced at her.

"Are you talking about science, or religion?"

Hannah paused. Then she could not help but smile – it was a good point, she supposed. Peter caught her expression and smiled briefly as well.

When they got to the cottage, Hannah walked beyond the building to the riverbank. The ground sloped gently down from the small cottage garden, right to the water's edge. She could imagine why Adriane had wanted to live here while she was researching, with her work right on her doorstep.

"My mother used to come out here and have tea with Adriane in the evenings," said Peter. "My sister would come too, and her children. Adriane would tell them about the plants and the fish. She knew everything by sight."

Looking at the peaceful shimmers on the water, it was hard to believe that something bad had happened to Adriane. Hannah sighed, before turning back to the cottage.

Inside, Hannah spent some time poking around, looking at the things Adriane had left behind. Mary had boxed them and left them where they were.

"So maybe she did have a habit of taking off and leaving things behind," said Hannah. "I guess she could have done the same thing again, when she left the trunk and letter at my friend's place..."

"I think she was supposed to come back for these things," said Peter. "My mother said she was keeping them for Adriane."

"But why leave them behind at all?" asked Hannah. "It's just a couple of boxes."

"The research group left very suddenly," said Peter, "after their argument."

Hannah looked up from the box.

"What argument?"

"They didn't say? I thought you said you spoke to the people on the team?" said Peter. "My mother didn't say what they fought about, just that Adriane came home very upset one day and said there had been yelling, She left a few days later."

"None of them said anything," said Hannah. "Why wouldn't they mention it? If she was kicked out of the group, she might have lost her PHD opportunity, that would be a reason for running away."

"Maybe they were lying to protect someone," said Peter.

"I thought your mother said they were 'nice'?" asked Hannah. "You disagree with her?"

"Nice and good aren't always the same," shrugged Peter.

"Don't I know it," muttered Hannah. "Sometimes I wonder if you can ever find someone who's both."

"I'd rather meet someone good than someone nice," said Peter.

For some reason Hannah could not define, she found herself sharing a smile with him again.

***

Hannah resisted the urge to throw her phone across the room.

She had spent almost three hours trying to get various people to talk to her. She had not expected much of a response from the police, after she shared the revelation that Adriane had argued with her colleagues before she died.

But still. They didn't even say that they would follow up.

So Hannah had followed up herself, calling each of Hannah's colleagues in turn. Each of them had either denied that an argument had taken place, or claimed that they didn't know what it was about.

Even the professor who had been supervising the study didn't know.

"Get enough people working closely together, and argument break out," he said, sighing. "Bioengineering is a competitive field."

"But weren't you all working together?" Hannah pressed. "Wouldn't you have shared credit?"

"It's not always that simple," was all Professor Browning would say.

Hannah then took some time to look at the discovery they had been working on, hoping for some enlightenment, but the science was beyond her. It looked like the team had been working on a way to grow a type of moss that had a natural painkiller when processed into medication. They had patented a way of engineering it, and the patent had been purchased by a pharmaceutical company last year for a vast sum of money.

Hannah sat staring at her phone, wondering what she might do next.

She wondered if she could go back to the farm. Peter had been clearly invested in helping her out, and she felt bad for judging him so harshly. No matter how much his religion looked down on outsiders, she should have known he would care about a possible crime.

She knew many of the Amish folk kept phones for emergencies. She should have asked for his number, when she left the other day. Would it be listed anywhere?

Before she could look, her phone started buzzing.

"Hello, Hannah? This is Peter. I hope you don't mind me calling."

"You called me? You're allowed to do that?"

"Not if it was just for a chat," said Peter, sounding as though he was smiling a little. "But this is important. Do you have news?"

Hannah went over her frustrating morning.

"They're still covering up," said Peter thoughtfully. "Then maybe this will help. I found another box that belonged to Adriane. It was in the loft. My sister Sarah visited this morning and reminded me of it."

"What's in it?"

"Notebooks. I can't understand most of it, and neither can Sarah, but we thought..."

"I'll be right over."

Hannah was in her car and driving before she had a chance to reconsider.

"They're never going to accept us," she could hear her mother saying, fifteen years ago, tears choking her. "We should have known. We're too different. There's no compromise."

Hannah drove until she had left the voices behind.

***

"I think I found something."

"Let me see."

Peter held up a sheet of paper, covered with scrawled notes in the same handwriting as the rest of the paper they had found in the box.

His sister, Sarah, passed the sheet over to Hannah, who laid it next to the rest of the papers they had placed along the workbench in Peter's barn. It looked like a to-do list, with some items crossed off. People to call, emails to send. Many of the notes could only have made sense to the one who wrote them.

Call S about confirming Type II barriers, meeting after morning brief.
Email reminder to group for x, fs and w5.
Sample pick up by Q or R if late.

The last note was written in a different pen to the others, large and scrawled, barely legible.

Call D about gnt q. Important!

On the top of the page was the date – the last day anyone had seen Adriane.

"This is the way she wrote in the letter," said Hannah. "Adriane. Her writing was messier and bigger, like she was in a hurry. She was agitated, or scared, I think."

I am coming to see you soon, Adriane had written in her letter to Peter's mother. *I've found out something that's been worrying me a lot. I can't stop thinking about what it might mean. You've always given me such good advice, Mary.*

"Do you think she meant Daisy?" asked Sarah. "Call Daisy? That's the only name beginning with D who is involved."

Hannah nodded. It felt so bizarre to be having this conversation in barn, with two people who looked like they had stepped out of a century long passed.

Sarah had waited with Peter for Hannah to arrive, and had greeted her as a friend. She had acted as though it was a given that she would be helping out, and had also claimed to have been a friend of Adriane's. Hannah wasn't sure what to make of it.

While Sarah went to go check on her kids, Hannah tried to call Daisy once more. There was no answer.

"I'll have to drive over and see her," she said, taking the piece of paper.

After a moment, she laid it back down again.

"What's the matter?" asked Peter.

"Maybe this is evidence," said Hannah. "If something did happen to Adriane, then this might be evidence. We should have worn gloves."

Peter looked down at the pages, tapping his chin with the tip of his finger.

"It seems like you want the police to be doing this."

"Of course I do," said Hannah, frowning.

"But don't you want to write about it?"

"Not you too," sighed Hannah. "I don't need to break the story – I mean, sure, that kind of thing is a big opportunity, but – it's a criminal case. I can't mess it up for the police."

"You're not what I expected," Peter said, looking at her with curiosity. "For a reporter."

"Oh, really?" said Hannah. "You thought I was trying to dig up dirt just to get a headline? Why bother helping me, then?"

"That's not what I meant," said Peter.

"It's fine. I don't expect you to give the outsider the benefit of the doubt," said Hannah, taking a picture of the piece of paper with her phone.

"It feels like you're the one standing in judgement," said Peter, stepping back. "I just offered to help."

"I – I know," said Hannah.

She calmed herself, glancing upward in frustration. She needed to keep a lid on her feelings.

"I'm sorry," she said. "It's nice of you to help. I guess you want to make sure we find your mom's friend."

"Partly," said Peter. "But it wasn't just her. Everyone still talks about Adriane. They wonder what happened."

"They do?"

Peter looked at her for a moment. Hannah bit her lip.

"I'm sorry," she said again.

"Here," Peter said, turning away suddenly and grabbing a scrap of paper.

He wrote the number for his emergency phone, as well as his name, and handed the paper over.

"In case something comes up," he said.

Hannah took it quickly, her cheeks burning. She knew the number was only for emergencies, but it still felt like a very personal gesture.

Leaving the barn, she nearly walked right into Sarah, who looked a little embarrassed. Hannah guessed that she had overheard.

"Thanks again for the help," said Hannah. "I'll let you guys know if I find anything."

"Thank you," smiled Sarah. "I'm sure you'll find out what happened. Peter said how smart you were."

"Not always that smart," said Hannah, still feeling heat on her cheeks.

The confusing warmth trailed her to her car. Why should it matter if Peter thought she was smart? Why would it matter that he had been hurt buy her judgements?

The answers to those questions were best avoided, Hannah thought.

***

Never pin your story on one source, Hannah reminded herself as she trudged back to her car.

This was a lesson she had learned early on. A story with only one source was useless, unless you could corroborate the information.

She had been pinning all her hopes on Daisy, Adriane's old friend. If the two of them had met on the day that Adriane had disappeared, Daisy might hold some clue.

Hannah had managed to catch Daisy as she left work for the day. Daisy had immediately denied seeing Adriane on that final day.

"She might have wanted to meet up, but she never sent me a message or anything," she had said, folding her arms over her coat and tapping one stiletto on the sidewalk.

Hannah had felt suspicious, wondering if Daisy might be lying. Perhaps something had happened...

But then Daisy had told Hannah that she had spent that day at meetings, trying to get funding for their project.

"I got it, too," she said. "You can ask Professor Browning. I used a discovery he made to get the grant, and we got enough funding to finish to research – you can see where it's gotten me."

She gestured behind her at the large building that housed the high-end pharmaceutical company she worked for.

Hannah got the feeling she had annoyed Daisy with her questions – this was confirmed by the phone call she received as she got into her car.

"Professor Browning, hi. What's going on?" Hannah put the phone on speaker as she pulled out and started driving.

"I just got a message from Daisy, saying I needed to confirm an alibi or something?" said the professor, in a slightly amused tone.

Hannah could imagine him laughing at the idea of her investigation. After such an abrupt dead end, she was rethinking everything herself.

"I was just checking something," she said. "I thought Daisy might have seen Adriane before she disappeared."

"I doubt it," said the professor. "They were barely speaking by the end of the summer."

"Really? I'd heard there were a few arguments in the group."

"There were, but it was mostly Adriane and Daisy. They were both natural leaders, and the clashed a great deal. I think they both wanted to be remembered for our discoveries."

"If Adriane wanted credit for your project, doesn't it seem strange to run off right when you were making progress?" asked Hannah, merging onto the highway.

"I'd assumed she was angry that Daisy was the one who managed to secure the grant," said the professor. "She didn't want second place. You understand – I'm sure journalism is just as competitive,"

Hannah declined to answer that.

"Are you going to write the story soon?" asked the professor.

"I don't have much to go on," said Hannah. "I've been working with the family who Adriane was staying with."

"The Amish farmers?" laughed the professor. "Goodness, that must be dull."

"Not to everyone, professor."

"Well, no, but surely to a city reporter like yourself."

Hannah bristled at his tone. She remembered seeing his picture – a middle aged, bespectacled man, who looked as though he had been born to lecture people. She could picture him laughing.

If she had been less annoyed, she might not have said what she did.

"I nearly converted."

"I beg your pardon?"

"When I was a teenager. My family was going to join the People. I was looking forward to it,"

"Really?"

The professor sounded disbelieving. Hannah couldn't blame him.

"Yep," she said. On hearing a buzz from her phone, she added, "got to go, I just got another message."

Her text-to-voice function read the message out as she drove.

"Meet me at Adriane's old cottage at eight. I have to tell you something. Daisy."

Hannah felt her heart speed up. She glanced at an upcoming sign, and realized she was already on her way back there.

For some reason, she had driven toward the Amish community, rather than going back home.

***

Hannah half-wished she had gone back to the farm to speak with Peter before coming out to the cottage. She had promised to keep him and Sarah up to date.

But she was embarrassed about the way she had acted. Weirdly, it felt like Peter was her friend now – and she had upset him.

And speaking with the professor earlier had brought back so many memories, now all the stronger as she sat at the edge of the river, waiting for eight o clock to arrive.

The evening was quiet, the sky above a pale lilac color as the sun sank below the hills. The scent of damp grass and nearby wildflowers filled the humid air. The birds were loud in their evening chorus.

Hannah could not help remembering the time when she had thought this would be her life.

It had been years back. Hannah's mother had met Aaron while working at the local market. There were plenty of Plain folk who sold goods there – Hannah's mother had made friends with several of them, but had not become close.

Aaron was different. He was a widower with no children, who was instantly smitten by the beautiful, quiet Englishwoman.

Hannah watched her mother fall in love over the course of just a few weeks, as the market's summer season brought her and Aaron together. Aaron had been wonderful to Hannah as well, always friendly and accepting.

After a while, Hannah's mother had asked whether Hannah might consider the two of them joining the People, and becoming a part of Aaron's family. She had expected teenaged Hannah to argue – and been surprised when she didn't.

Hannah had been entranced by the idea of becoming Amish. She had researched everything she could, learning about the culture and rules. She had always gone to church with her mother, but for the first time she felt like she had found a life where she could be the person God had designed her to be.

They had all been so excited.

And then Aaron had come to them, one day, and told them that he had spoken to the community leaders about his plan.

He had not needed to go into detail, his expression making it clear enough. It did not matter that Hannah's mother was willing to convert fully, and follow the *Ordnung* to the letter. The community was not willing to accept the outsiders.

Looking around at the quiet evening, Hannah tried to block out the memories of the heartbreak.

That had been years ago. Besides, the Amish community Aaron had belonged to had been one of the most conservative in the area.

If they had wanted to join this place – where people were willing to be friends even if you didn't belong – would it have been different?

Why do you feel like you belong here? she thought she could hear Someone say.

I don't belong here, she answered. *I was wrong.*

But why could she still see herself here? Living this life?

Why did she still want to walk back over the farm and see Peter again?

Hannah glanced up. The birds had stopped singing.

She got to her feet, glancing at her phone – it was five past eight. Something rustled behind her.

Before she could turn, she was thrown forward by a sudden, stunning blow to her shoulder, at the same time as an unthinkably loud crack split the air behind her. She fell, her temple striking a rock.

She didn't register that the noise had been a gunshot until she was already lying on the ground, staring at her hands in the long grass and taking in a huge gulp of air. Warmth blossomed from her shoulder, and a sickly feeling flooded across her chest.

Whoever had shot her was still moving, feet crunching on the pebbles and dirt. Hannah braced her weight on her hands and kicked out behind her. She felt her heel connect with something. There was a cracking sound, a hiss of pain, and a dry thud as someone landed in the grass.

Hannah scrambled to her feet and started running. When she reached the cottage, she turned back for a moment, hand held to the wound on her shoulder.

Whoever had attacked her was still on the ground, hidden by the tall river grass and tree shadows. They were moving, however – she turned and ran on.

***

The pain had still not caught up with Hannah when she reached Peter's door. Her hands and head felt numb, and she was looking down in surprise at the blood on her palms when Peter answered.

"What on earth – what happened?"

Peter's face was white as he stepped aside to let Hannah in., eyes roaming from the blood on her shirt to the bruise on the side of her head.

"We need to call the police," she told him.

"Who did this?" Peter stepped close, peeling back the torn fabric of her sleeve to see her shoulder. "It's not deep, it just a graze," he said in obvious relief.

"Okay. Okay." Hannah took a deep breath. "I didn't see who it was, I was by the river, I didn't see them. I just ran up – oh, no, wait, they might have followed me."

Hannah shook her head. She was having trouble thinking, and her dizziness was finally starting to register as pain. She moved back to the door.

"I should go, they might have followed me, it's not safe."

Peter held the door closed as she tried to open it, her hand slipping on the latch. He handed her a folded up handkerchief, indicating that she should press it against her shoulder.

"Hold on," he said. "I don't think you should be moving. Let me just call the police, and –"

"You can't go out to the barn, I came that way – they might be following me," Hannah said again, trying to make her words more distinct. "They have a gun. They have a gun, they shot me."

"I know, Hannah," said Peter gently. "Did you hear them coming after you?"

Hannah squinted at Peter. Suddenly the light from the lamps in the hall seemed very bright.

"I don't know. It's not safe," she said. "We're not safe." Why was it so hard to make sense?

Peter took a deep breath, still visibly shaken.

"We'll go to Sarah's," he said. "It's a ten minute walk."

"Okay. Okay. Good."

Hannah managed to get the door open and immediately stumbled over the threshold.

"Wait – Hannah – this is ridiculous –"

Hannah heard Peter following her down the porch steps.

"You can't walk like this."

"I'll be fine. You said five minutes. I'll be fine." Hannah stared at her hands again, which were now out of focus. "My shoulder feels weird. And my head hurts."

Everything drifted for a few moments. Hannah was vaguely aware of Peter's gentle suggestion that he carry her, and her accepting, and then being lifted up.

"You'll have to be quiet," she muttered, holding a hand to her shoulder. "They might see us."

"They won't, it's getting dark. We'll cut across the pasture." Peter's voice was low. He sounded afraid. Hannah was glad of this – it meant he knew the danger was real. "What were you doing by the river?"

"I was supposed to meet Daisy. She sent me a message."

"Daisy did this?"

"I don't know." Hannah frowned, trying to concentrate. "Maybe. She might want to shut me up. I found out she was fighting with Adriane, before she died."

"You think Adriane died?" asked Peter. "You're sure?"

"Why else would someone do this?" asked Hannah. "I knew she was dead. I knew from the start."

"I thought so too," said Peter sadly.

After a moment, Hannah closed her eyes, the motion of the trees making her feel nauseated.

"I'm sorry," she said.

"Why do you have to be sorry for? You're the one who's been hurt."

"But whoever it is will probably come after us. And now you're not safe. I'm sorry." Hannah sighed. "I kept saying that I wasn't following this story for me, that I was doing it to get the truth, but honestly – I did keep thinking about what it would do for my career."

"Is that so bad?"

"If I've put you in danger for myself, then yes, it is," Hannah said. "I don't even care about my stupid career, or not like I'm supposed to. And I've dragged you into this, and now we're going to drag Sarah into it as well."

"Don't worry about that right now," said Peter.

They continued walking for a few moments. Hannah discovered that closing her eyes made the nausea worse. She kept them open instead, staring at the darkened fields, distracting herself from the pain that now seemed to be coming from everywhere at once.

It was still hard to think. Peter was not saying anything, looking ahead. Hannah looked up at the point of his chin, the worried line of his mouth.

"We're friends, right?" Hannah asked.

"I'd like to think so. I wasn't sure if you'd want to be friends with someone who was Amish."

"I was being a jerk. It's not your fault." Hannah didn't even hesitate before telling him the truth – though whether this was because of the danger they were in, or because of the blow to the head, she could not be sure. "I wanted to be Amish."

"You did?"

"Me and my mom. We were going to join, but they wouldn't let us,"

"Oh. I'm so sorry."

"Not your fault. Anyway, you and Sarah, you're different. This place seems different. More open."

"We still keep ourselves from the outside world. But we can't keep God's love from anyone. That's the point."

"Yeah. That is. Or it should be." Hannah looked up at the stars. *God's love.* Was that what she was feeling? Was that the connection she felt with Peter? "I'm not making sense."

"It's all right," said Peter. "We're nearly there."

"I don't like it when I can't think properly."

"You're very smart most of the time, I'm sure it will even out in the end," said Peter, sounding as though he was smiling.

"Yeah. You told Sarah I was smart," said Hannah, smiling too.

Peter did not answer, but suddenly started coughing like he needed to clear his throat.

"Are you holding up okay?" Hannah asked. "Do you need to take a break?"

"Well – I guess. Just for a moment," said Peter, lowering her to sit on the grass.

The sun was gone by now, their path lit by just a sliver of moonshine. Hannah looked back, wondering if her attacker had followed them. Would he or she be able to see them in the moonlight?

"Oh, wait, I just realised – can't you call the police on your cell phone?" said Peter, leaning into a stretch with his hands against the small of his back.

"I dropped the phone by the river," mumbled Hannah. "I hope it's not broken."

"That's not the biggest worry at the moment, surely."

"No worry at all, to be honest, but it's so inconvenient to have to replace everything. All my contacts."

"You don't have them written down?" asked Peter.

"Only yours," said Hannah, pulling the piece of paper with his emergency number from her jacket pocket and waving it in the air proudly.

It was hard to tell in the dark, but she thought Peter might be smiling,

"I'm sorry I didn't get to meet you before," said Hannah, lying back onto the cold grass.

"What do you mean?"

"I mean if I'd been Amish. If I'd converted, I might have met you years ago." Hannah lifted the paper over her face, studying it closely. "We might have been friends."

"You said we already were friends," said Peter quietly.

There was a pause.

"You know what I mean," said Hannah, still unable to be anything but honest.

"I do," he replied. He drew a hand over his face. "And I – I'm sorry, but I wish you hadn't told me, about wanting to become Amish."

"It would be easier to know there had never been any chance for us," said Hannah, nodding. "Yeah. You're right. I'm sorry. Pretend I didn't say anything, okay?"

There was quiet for a moment.

Then Hannah sat up so quickly she set her head spinning again.

"Look! Peter, look at this!"

"What?" Peter looked at the paper she held out. "It's just my name and the phone number for the farm."

"No, I mean the way you wrote your name. Look at the P. It's all big and loopy."

"So?"

"So it looks like a D."

Hannah pointed at the letter in question. Peter's writing was large and sprawling, like Adriane's had been when she was writing in an agitated state.

"What if Adriane was writing about meeting someone who began with a P?" she said. "Not Daisy?"

"No-one she worked with had a name beginning with P," said Peter, frowning.

"Unless you go by your official title. I'll bet Browning made everyone call him Professor."

Peter considered this for a moment.

"What would his reason be for hurting her?"

"I don't know. Maybe something to do with the grant – Daisy used his work for the application. If his work was wrong, they would have lost the money. If Adriane found something out, he might have wanted to silence her."

Peter shivered. "All right. Maybe. Let's get going, and we'll tell the police when we call them from Sarah's."

Hannah felt more alert for the second part of the journey, enough to start feeling the first hints of embarrassment of being carried like a child. However, she knew Peter would be feeling even more awkward, and decided not to say anything.

She wished she could focus on the beauty of the surrounding night, but she was starting to feel nauseated once more. When they finally reached Sarah's home, Hannah asked to be put down again.

"We're nearly at the door," said Peter.

"No, I think I'm going to be sick. Please."

Peter obligingly placed Hannah down on a stretch of grass at the front of the house, just below the porch. He walked up the steps – and then stopped short, his breath catching.

Before Hannah could ask what was wrong, the door opened.

"Peter – what on earth's the matter?" Sarah's voice was concerned.

"Who's this?" asked Peter, his voice slightly louder than it should have been.

"Professor Browning. He used to work with Adriane."

Hannah's heart dropped.

"Hello, you must be Peter," said a thin, reedy voice that Hannah recognized from her phone conversations. "I heard there was an investigation into Adriane's disappearance, and I hoped there might be news."

Hannah crawled over to the side of the porch, pressing herself against the wooden boards so there was no chance anyone standing at the front door could see her.

"Peter?" Sarah spoke uncertainly. "What's wrong? Is that – is that blood on your shirt?"

"It's Hannah," said Peter slowly. "Someone attacked her."

"Oh my goodness, is she alright?" asked the professor.

"No." Peter paused. "She was dead when I found her."

Sarah let out a soft gasp of shock. Another voice, presumably belonging to Sarah's husband, chimed in from the behind the others.

"Have you called the police?"

"The phone in the barn isn't working," said Peter. Hannah heard him step forward. "I need to use yours."

Hannah readied herself to crawl around the side of the house, and meet Peter out back by the phone. But the professor had already interrupted.

"I have a cell phone, I'll call. The poor girl, I can't imagine what happened."

"Something to do with her story?" asked Sarah, as the professor stepped onto the porch to make the call.

Hannah listened in silence as he reported her murder.

The others were just inside, beyond the open door. Peter, Sarah, and Sarah's husband. And the children would be upstairs, asleep.

All Hannah could think about was the gun.

Peter needed to get the others out, and away from the professor. But how to do that without arousing suspicion? Could they just fake it until the police arrived, and they were safe?

"Hey, Aaron?" Hannah heard Peter say, as the professor ended the call. "Can I borrow a clean shirt?"

"Sure," said Hannah's husband.

Perfect, Hannah thought. Peter could get Aaron alone, and tell him what was happening – but then Sarah spoke up.

"Hannah kept talking about keeping evidence clean," she said. "Might the police want you to leave it on? I know it's upsetting, but it might be important."

"That's a good point," said Aaron. "They'll be here soon, and you can ask them."

"Right," said Peter slowly. "Sure."

"So you were helping Hannah with her story, then?" asked the professor.

Hannah's blood ran cold at the question. The little group was just inside the house, and the front door was still open. She pressed herself harder against the side of the porch, ignoring the pain in her shoulder.

"We helped her go through those notes we found, that belonged to Adriane," said Sarah. Her voice was pitching, like she was trying not to cry. "Oh, Hannah, I can't believe it."

"Yes, it's a tragedy," agreed the professor. "But so good of you to try and help. I didn't know Adriane had left notes behind. What did they say?"

"We couldn't understand them," Peter said quickly.

"Most of them, we couldn't," said Sarah. "There were a few things about meetings that seemed clear. And there were some notes about the arguments Adriane was having."

"Were there, now?" asked the professor.

Come on, Peter, Hannah thought. *Change the subject. He's going to realize you know the truth –*

"I looked over them as well," Aaron said. "I was actually thinking that the arguments might have been to do with the grant."

"What grant?" asked the professor, his voice sharp.

"It doesn't matter now, surely," said Peter.

"The police might need to know," said Aaron. "Adriane kept using letters instead of words. I thought when she wrote g-n-t it might mean grant."

"Maybe," said Peter. "It might also be some science thing. Sarah, I think I need some tea, would you mind?"

"Of course," said Sarah.

There were the sounds of two sets of footsteps, heading to the kitchen.

"Hold on." The professor's voice rang out. "Peter, you seem a little nervous."

He knows, Hannah thought. *He knows that Peter knows the truth.*

"Just upset," tried Peter. "I just need to –"

From the gasps that followed, it was evident that the professor had taken his gun out.

"What are you doing?"

"That's quite a lot of blood, Peter," said the professor. "Hannah was dead when you found her, you said? No time for last minute confessions?"

There was no reply.

"She was just like Adriane," the professor continued. "Wouldn't stop pushing, even when there was nothing to be found. Adriane got it in her head that we didn't deserve the grant we had won for our research. Everyone lies in grant applications, it's practically expected. But she wouldn't leave it alone, especially after she had been talking with your mother about all that religious nonsense all summer."

Peter cleared his throat.

"Professor, if you leave now, you can get away before the police arrive."

"But I'm the one who called them. And they're going to wonder where I went. No, no, I think that a better story would be that Daisy, having killed your friend, came up here and tried to cover her tracks. I fought her off, but only after she had killed you. Very tragic."

"You killed Hannah," breathed Sarah. "And – and Adriane."

"Like I said, they were very much alike. Both of them even fell for the same trick, responding to a message to meet in private. At the exact same spot, would you believe?"

He would only be telling them this if he had already decided to kill them, Hannah thought.

And now she got to choose. She could feel that pull, the same one that had brought her back here. The little voice in her head that she had tried so hard to silence.

Had she really meant it, when she had spoken to Peter just a few minutes ago? When she had regretted bringing his family into danger?

If they were worth protecting, then that was what she needed to do. She didn't have a choice.

She pushed herself up off the cool grass, holding onto the side of the porch as she got to her feet. She staggered to the middle of the yard, within sight of the front door.

She could see the professor, with his back to her, and the others, further into the room.

"Hey," she called out. Her voice was hoarse, and didn't carry. "*Hey,*" she tried again, louder.

The professor turned.

"I'm not as much like Adriane as you thought," she yelled. "I'm still alive."

"Hannah, don't," Peter shouted out.

The professor had already started running, his gun held out. Peter and Aaron started after him – Hannah turned and made for the gate that led to the road.

Two more shots rang out, missing Hannah as she ran. She kept moving, into the road and towards the corner.

With every step, she expected to be thrown forward again, and this time not to rise back up.

She didn't even see the lights on the police car until she had rounded the corner and nearly ran right into it.

It managed to stop just in time. The passenger door swung open, and a familiar face appeared.

"What on earth –" Detective Brenner stared at Hannah.

Hannah waved back weakly. Having stopped running, she was no longer able to stand, and ended up dropping down onto a grass bank at the side of the road.

"That way," she managed, pointing in the direction of the house. "He has a gun. Professor Browning, he –"

The detective wasted no time in sprinting in the direction she was pointing. Hannah closed her eyes, listening to the other officers following the detective, and the shouts that came afterward. There were no shots, however, and eventually everything became quiet. Hannah couldn't tell what was going on.

After a while, she stopped trying.

***

Hannah didn't realize how bright the hospital ward lights were until she opened her eyes and looked directly into them.

They did not keep her attention for long, however, when she saw who was sitting in the chair next to her bed.

"You scared me half to death," said Peter.

"Sorry," said Hannah, bringing her hand up to the bandages on her shoulder. "I'll make it up to you."

Peter rolled his eyes, but he was smiling a little. He told her about what had happened after she had passed out – how the police had caught Browning alive, and he had told them where he had buried Adriane.

He also let her know that Sarah and Aaron were fine, and wanted to visit – as did Detective Brenner, who was trying very hard to act like she wasn't embarrassed by what had happened.

"You'll have a big story to write," Peter said. "If you want it. And you caught a killer."

Hannah sighed.

"Yes, we did," she said. "But I don't think I want the story. At all."

No, she didn't want it. She hadn't wanted it from the start – it had been that voice inside her, telling her to find the truth, that had driven her on.

The same voice that she could now hear.

Well done, my child.

Hannah felt herself tearing up. The voice had never gone away, she knew that now. God had always been there.

"You don't want to write?" asked Peter.

"I do," said Hannah. "But I'm not sure what about. I think I'll take a while and work that out."

"And in the meanwhile?"

Hannah took a deep breath.

Be brave, the voice told her.

"You remember when I told you to forget I said anything about wanting to be Amish? That it was easier to pretend there was no chance for us?" she asked.

Peter nodded.

"I think I've changed my mind," Hannah said.

Peter looked at her for a moment. "You – you want to become Amish?"

"Yes."

"That's a big decision," he said slowly. "You can't make it for – for a single person."

"I made the decision a long time ago," said Hannah. "I'm just making it again."

This is the life I meant for you. It's been waiting.

"What you do with the information is up to you, of course," she added.

Peter looked at her with raised eyebrows, before breaking into a wide smile.

"I know exactly what I'm going to do, darling," he said.

THE AMISH ROMANCE OF NIKKI HAMILTON

Nikki Hamilton had no idea what was about to happen when she decides it was time to discover her past. After her mother's passing, she discovers that she was born Amish. She now wants to know why her mother left the life she was born into. Her adventure to River Stone turns out to be quite an eye opener and she soon discovers that there is a peace there that she would never be able to have in the city. When she meets John Smith, a local farmer from Trumbull, everything changes, and for the first time since her arrival, she's contemplating her future.

John had lost his wife three years ago, and he never once thought that he would ever fall in love again. But against all odds he meets the intriguing Nikki Hamilton, an Englischer with a passion for writing novels. She is eccentric and different, but even with these obstacles and the fact that she's not Amish, he can't keep himself from falling in love. But they are from two different worlds. Is she willing to become Amish?

Translations:

Baremlich = Terrible
Gleh vennigh or gleh bissley — little bit.
Jah – yes

Chapter 1

The tiny creature zoomed about the room like a firefly on steroid. And as small as it was, it wreaked havoc in Clara's tiny little room high up in the attic of the old Steinberg mansion. Down below she could hear the hurried footsteps of Mrs Meremoth, the housekeeper. She grabbed one of her books and swatted at the firefly but it evaded her every move. As it zoomed over her small desk it sent papers flying in all directions. And as

Clara was about to burst out in tears everything slowed down. The papers hung in a suspended state in the air and even Mrs Meremoth's footsteps had grown quiet.

Clara fell back on her bed that stood against the wall next to the window and the tiny creature with humanlike features and wings like that of a fly perched on her windowsill.

Awestruck she crawled closer. "Who are you?" she whispered.

"I am Hefeydd, King of the Fae," he announced with his hands planted on his sides.

Clara gasped and her eyes grew wide with wonder. "I don't understand you can't possibly be real." said Clara to the infinitesimal figure perched on her windowsill.

The winged creature laughed, and his laughter shook the window panes despite his miniature size.

"So trifling human girl! Your feeble minds can hardly correlate all the facts and fallacies of your own existence, and you dare doubt ours?"

Clara's brows drew together like the London Tower bridge over the Thames river....

Nikki's fingers flew over the keys of her laptop, she had finally gotten over the writer's block that had been the bane of her existence over the past few weeks, and suddenly her screen died.

"No, no, no, no!" she cried out and banged her hands on the desk. "This cannot be happening!"

She scurried around to find her power supply which she so carelessly discarded earlier when she returned from the library. If she stops now, she's going to lose her inspiration.

She jumped up and hopped on one foot while putting on one shoe then on the other while she tossed the clothes that lay on her bed in all direction searching for her power supply. If she hurried she could get to the market before nightfall to charge her laptop and her power bank. Being it the only place with actual electricity, she had to hurry. Here at her aunt Eva's home in the middle of River Stone, a small Amish village, she was at the mercy of the elements. Other than running water and coal stove, there wasn't really anything, but that was a sacrifice she had been willing to make after discovering her roots.

Shortly after her mother's passing she had discovered that her mother grew up here in River Stone and that she had run away just after her eighteenth birthday and started a life for herself in New Jersey. With her discovery, Nikki couldn't quench her curiosity about this her mother's mysterious past. Since she could remember, her mother never once mentioned her family, which she found odd. Her mother's past had always been a mystery, and it was one she had vowed to unravel against her father's wishes.

With backpack and all, she rushed down the stairs and past her aunt.

"Nicola, where are you going?"

"It's Nikki Aunt Eva, Nikki with a double K and I'm just going to the market real quick."

For the life of her she couldn't understand why her aunt insisted on calling her Nicola when her name was Nikki.

"But it's almost lunch time dear," her aunt protested.

"I'll be back soon, I promise," Nikki persisted and rushed out the door.

There was no way anyone was going to prevent her from getting her laptop charged. She was already committed to spend the evening writing so that she could get this Novel done and stopping now will set her back at least a day. A deadline was a deadline.

John was about half a mile away from the market, his carriage loaded with fruits and vegetables from his farm back in Trumbull when suddenly his carriage jerked and his horses stalled. It was already past lunch time, and he had hoped to be at the market almost two hours ago. But delays on the road, had kept him, and now on top of it, the carriage wheel had separated from the carriage. Frustrated, he got off and walked around to the right side of the carriage to inspect the damage. He really didn't expect this to happen, but then again, he hardly did any maintenance on his carriages. When he didn't farm, he spent his days behind books reading, anything from historical books to modern Englisch biographies. This will teach him, he thought disappointedly. He was going to have to walk the rest of the way to River Stone and find one of the locals to come and help him.

He had just collected his belongings when the sound of a scooter drew closer, in the distance he could see the rider was a female, but the way her hair waved in the wind from under the helmet. It was obvious by her clothes that she was also an Englischer. Not expecting much help, he turned and started to walk but instead of the rider whizzing past she stopped.

"Do you need any help?" she asked from behind the visor.

"Um, I don't think so, my wheel split I just need to get to River Stone market."

The woman removed her helmet and John held his breath. She was beautiful, he was not going to deny that, but he knew better than to want.

"I can give you a ride; I'm heading to the market, anyway."

John contemplated this; he was losing time as it was, and if he could get to the market sooner than later, he could at least find someone to help him before night fall. He glanced at the scooter and then back at his wagon filled with fruit and vegetables.

"If it's no trouble," he said tentatively.

She waved her hand and smiled, "No problem at all, hop on."

John awkwardly moved to get on the back of the scooter, with little space he was sitting up against her back with his hands on her shoulders.

"Hold on," she warned tend put her helmet back on before starting her scooter.

As she pulled away, he jerked and nearly flew off the back but managed to regain his grip. Within twenty minutes or so, they reached River Stone and the young woman pulled to a stop near the warehouse.

"Well, here we are," she said and waited for him to get off, before she got off.

"Thank you."

"No problem."

And without waiting she dashed into the warehouse.

What an odd character, he thought as he watched her disappear. She was completely out of place here at River Stone, yet she seemed like she was comfortable among the Amish. He couldn't help but wonder if she was some sort of reporter who like so many, visited Amish villages to get a scoop on their lives.

"I see you've met Eva's niece."

"Abraham!" John greeted and shook his friend's hand, "She's not Amish though."

"No, she isn't, not yet anyway, but she's made herself at home."

Abraham chuckled and crossed his arms. "So pray tell, how on earth did you manage to get on the back of that thing?"

John rubbed the back of his head and sighed. "My carriage broke down about a two miles outside of town. And this young lady came to my rescue."

"I see, well, let's go and get your produce, and I'll arrange for one of my boys to go see to the carriage and the horses."

"Thanks."

The two men were off in no time, but John couldn't get the red head out of his mind. She intrigued him, and he wanted to find out more about her.

Chapter 2

The warehouse was more like a local grocer; the walls were lined with shelves containing various preserved items like preserved lemons, apricots, beans, and mixed veggies. And of course her favourite, sweet and sour preserved figs. Towards the back of the warehouse were homemade dresses and tea towels, quilted blankets and cute little doilies with beaded edges. Something she had never seen in her life, but Aunt Eva used them over all her containers in her kitchen.

She darted for the counter and plastered her most amiable smile on her face.

"Good afternoon Mrs Troyer, isn't it a lovely day today?"

Mrs Troyer raised a brow, but a smile tugged at the corners of her mouth. "Indeed, it's a lovely day to spend outside and get to meet a few people."

Nikki cringed inwardly. Mrs Troyer had been trying to get her more involved at the market, but right now she had a deadline.

"I promise by Friday I'll be out and about, I just need to finish the last few chapters of my book, would I be able to use your power again?"

"Nikki, you should put that thing away and take time to get to know the surrounding people. You bury your face in that monstrosity and it isn't good."

Nikki sighed and bit her lip, "I know, I just need to get my work done before I can actually spend time enjoying this wonderful place."

Mrs Troyer wiped her hand on her apron and gestured with her head. "I'll be closing shop early, so don't waste any time."

"Oh thank you! I really owe you big time."

Nikki headed to the back where she could plug her laptop in. She felt bad for using Mrs Troyer's electricity but every time she offered to pay, Mrs Troyer wanted to hear nothing of it. But she was adamant to contribute one way or the other. As soon as her book was finished, she promised herself she would come and give Mrs Troyer a hand and help her to stock up her shelves or something.

She settled behind her laptop and continued to write her book. It amazed her how her writers block had flown out the window the day she arrived here at River Stone. Back home, there were far too many distractions. Her apartment block was one of the rowdiest places, with couples squabbling on either side of her. Above her, her neighbours sounded like they were doing Irish dancing on wooden floors. Just after her mother's passing, she had learned that her mum used to be Amish. It was all in a letter her mum had left behind for her. From that she had learned that her mother left River Stone shortly after her sixteenth birthday when she couldn't take living here anymore. She had been on her Rumspringa and had met a young man, whom she had fallen in love with at the time. Completely smitten she was willing to sacrifice her life in the Amish community to explore the possibilities of modern life. It never worked out with this young man, but her mother refused to go back to her former life, and ended up staying in Ohio, where she eventually met her dad. This too didn't work out as planned. Shortly after her birth, her biological father ran off with some floozy and her mother was left to raise her all on her own. With no real education other than the minimal schooling she had here in River Stone, her mother worked two jobs at the local Walmart and coffee shop, just so that Nikki could go to school and finally study further. Her mother really gave her all and for that she was grateful. But Nikki couldn't help but wonder what it would have been like if her mum returned when she was still a baby.

Knowing that she could have grown up Amish, had her wonder what her life would have been like. It took her almost a year to track Aunt Eva down, and when she did, she impulsively jumped at the opportunity to find out for herself, why her mother decided that modern life was far better than the Amish. The information she had gathered the weeks before she finally packed her bag, was all hearsay. Articles on websites and blogs that sounded a little farfetched, not to mention the whole conspiracy that the Amish believe that the earth is flat, and that the devil hides in every electronic device.

Three hours later, she had finished the last few chapters of her book. Her creativity was blossoming, and all it needed now was editing. She attached her document in her email to her editor and sent it off.

Now, she could finally just relax and as Mrs Troyer insisted, experience the Amish life.

She glanced around her and her eyes fell on a lilac dress hanging on one of the rails. Maybe she should embrace the life in full for a while, walk in her mother's footsteps and see for herself what the Amish were about.

Chapter 3

The various stalls lined the market place and John was pleased that he had managed to get all his fresh produce here in time. It was the second day since he arrived, and despite the rain that had been pouring down none stop, he had made good revenue on his sales. By the end of the week he would have enough money to purchase more wood to build his shed back home. His heart cramped in his chest. To this day, three years after his wife's passing he still felt the tug in his heart when he thought of her. Mary always wanted a shed where she could work on her paintings, and he had promised to build her one for years, but never had the means. It was his promise to her at the time of her death that he would finish the shed as he promised.

"It's a *baremlich* day!" Abraham exclaimed as he ducked in under the cover where John has his stand.

"*Gleh vennigh or gleh bissley,* but we should be thankful for the rain."

"*Jah* I guess we need the rain. So have you sold much?"

"*Jah*, plenty, it's been a good season."

Abraham grinned and picked up one of the red starling apples, "Das gut, "he said and took a bite. "So will you be staying here much longer?"

John nodded, "Until the end of the week, but I will be back at the end of the month."

"Good to know, so you can join us for the grain harvest."

John grinned, he enjoyed those gatherings most of all. It's when everyone in the area gets together and helps with the thrashing. It's one of the annual events where everyone gets to frolic and enjoy each other's company.

"I'll definitely be here then."

"Excuse me," a woman's voice sounded behind him and when he turned around he was caught slightly off guard.

The young woman who helped him just yesterday stood before him wearing a Lilac dress with a white apron and a cap. She was quaintly transformed from Englisch to Amish and his heart impulsively skipped a beat. Abraham cleared his throat and made some random excuse to escape leaving him alone with the woman.

"How may I help you?" he asked attempting to sound casual.

"I see you managed to get your stuff here," she said smiling.

"Jah, I did. Thank you for bringing me to town."

"Oh it wasn't a bother at all."

Her smile lit up her grey eyes, and he had to force himself to look away, the last time he had noticed a woman was when he first met Mary, and having these feelings towards a complete stranger felt oddly out of place.

"Are you here to buy fruits or vegetables?" he asked curiously.

She smiled and looked at the crates. "Yes, I'm actually looking for some carrots and potatoes. Aunt Eva said I must come and see you."

"Well then I can most certainly help you there."

John reached for a woven basket and handed it to her. "Feel free to help yourself; the carrots are nice and sweet."

"I wouldn't know the first thing about vegetables," she said, and he noticed the slight blush on her cheeks.

"Right, well, it's all ripe and ready."

John bent down and picked up a bunch of carrots, "Did Eva say how many she wanted?"

"Oh... no she just said I must get some."

"Well why don't you take two bunches, they will last at least two weeks if she doesn't use it all today. And then a bag of potatoes will last her a while too."

"My name is Nikki Hamilton, by the way," she introduced.

Embarrassed he dusted his hands off and extended one hand to her, "I'm sorry, it was rude of me. My name is John."

"Just John?" she asked taking his hand.

"John Smith."

"Well John Smith, it's a pleasure to meet your acquaintance. How much do I owe you?"

John rambled off the amount and Nikki paid him. She was about to turn and leave when he jumped at the opportunity.

"Here let me help you."

"Oh no, it's fine, I'm parked all the way at the warehouse."

She sounded surprised, and he smiled. "It's fine, the stuff is heavy, I'll carry it for you."

"But you can't leave your stall unattended."

He frowned amusedly, realizing that she was worried about his goods.

"Yes I can," he smiled and flipped the sign board that read '*Be back in 15 min*'.

"What if your produce goes missing?" she asked alarmed and clung to her basket.

"My dear, this is not the city, people here are honest and they don't steal from the hand that feeds them."

By the surprised look on her face, he could tell she was amused. So he gently pried the basket from her hand and waited for her to follow him.

"I must admit, seeing you in Amish clothes is rather odd."

Nikki raised a brow and laughed, "Well I figured if I'm going to experience the Amish ways, I can't hold back."

The way John smiled caused a flutter in her stomach and she could feel a blush flood her cheeks.

"If you really want to experience an Amish adventure, you should get rid of your scooter."

"Oh heavens no, how will I get around?"

"You need a horse drawn buggy."

She laughed then. "Me driving a buggy, I doubt that would end well."

"Why so?"

"I'm afraid of horses," she admitted, "Or they are afraid of me, either way, we don't get along."

"I highly doubt that's the case, you just need to understand them."

They reached her scooter, and John took the liberty to fasten her basket on the carry rack on the back. She was keenly aware of him, and couldn't help but find him rather attractive although he was dressed very simple with his broadfall pants, blue shirt and suspenders. But there was something about him, something she couldn't quite put her finger on. His eyes were a deep brown and there was sadness in his eyes, but his smile was genuine.

Chapter 4

It had been a week since Nikki had met John, and he had gone on his way, back to his home town. But for some reason she couldn't get him out of her mind. He was so unlike the men she knew back home. He was kind, hospitable and a true gentleman. Taking into account that her most recent failed relationship had been with a body builder who had a bad attitude, meeting John was like the flip side of the coin.

"Aunt Eva?" she said one morning when they were having breakfast.

"Yes dear?"

"How well did you know my mother?"

Aunt Eva got up and took her dishes to the sink. "Your mother was a free spirit, she didn't believe in the restrictions of the Amish ways."

"And do you believe in these restrictions?"

Her aunt came to sit with her. "I'm still here," she smiled. "Your mother was young, and foolish. She chased after things of the world and I can't blame her. When we went on our Rumspringa, she met a boy, and she was instantly infatuated by his promises."

Nikki cupped the mug in her hands and looked at the coppery tea with the lemon floating inside of it. If this place had been so peaceful why would her mother have chosen another path? She thought about the things she had experienced thus far; friendly faces, casual frolics with the other Amish girls and learning, for the first time, how to quilt. Life here in this small Amish village was just too peaceful, it simply made no sense.

She sat quietly for a while and Aunt Eva started clearing the dishes.

"Will you be coming to church with me?" she asked.

Nikki nodded, "Sure, is it this evening?"

"Yes, at around six tonight, I think you'll enjoy it."

Her aunt was so excited, if she had to compare Eva to her mother, they were two completely different people.

"I'm sure it will be fun, what are your plans today?" she asked.

"I'm going to Mary to finish a few quilts; you're welcome to come along."

Nikki smiled and shook her head, she had other plans. There was a room in the house that was totally deserted. Aunt Eva made sure to keep the door closed at all times, and it was off limits for her, but perhaps she can find some more information about her mother and why she left in that room.

As soon as Aunt Eva had left, Jane made her way up the stairs to the top floor. Naturally her adrenalin was pumping as she approached the room at the end of the hallway. She slowly turned the door knob, and the door swung open. The curtains were drawn, and the room was covered in dust. On the small desk to the left of the tidy bed stood a vase with dead flowers, and next to it was a post card. Nikki leaned over, careful not to disturb the current state of the room and looked at the postcard. She couldn't make out what it said, it was written in Dutch, but at the bottom of the postcard was her mother's name with a small heart drawn next to it. The only thing she could make out was that it was addressed to Eva.

She looked around and tried to find more clues as to why her mother left, but there was nothing of value. Other than a normal few items of clothing, and books, it seemed like her mother has a very normal life. She was about to leave the room when she noticed the corner of a poster sticking out behind the closet. She carefully moved the closet away from the wall and reached behind it. It was an A4 sized poster of the Annie stage production at Broadway 1992—two years before she was born. On the border of the poster was scribbled—*I will go there.* The handwriting was the same as that on the post card.

It all suddenly made sense. Her mother must have seen this play and decided that the glamour of the city was far more appealing than the Amish life she had led. Once she had come to that conclusion she quietly left her mother's room and closed the door behind her. She had to admit, she half expected something far more sinister to come from this, but all it was, was that her mother had a dream, and she gave up her life to follow her dream. Not that she became a famous actress, but she got to see the world.

Chapter 5

As the days passed, Nikki's impatience for feedback from her editor started to dissipate more and more. Her phone now discarded in the bedside drawer next to her bed, and her laptop forgotten in the back of the wardrobe. She'd become more involved with the community, visiting the local school, joining in on various events hosted by the women in the community, and her weekly visit to church and frolicking sings had become the pinnacle of her everyday life here in River Stone. For the first time in her life, she wasn't chasing after impossible deadlines and annoying editors who insisted on show rather than tell scenes, especially when showing was completely irrelevant in the progress of the plot. But needless to say, her keen interest in a certain member of the Amish community was also the reason she so thoroughly enjoyed everything. John Smith, although not from River Stone, was an esteemed member nonetheless and there was something about him that intrigued Nikki. He was soft spoken with impeccably refined manners, which was in total contrast of his strong manly features. She could spend hours just watching him at his stall, loading heavy crates of fruits and vegetables into buyers' buggies. Every now and again she had to force herself not to stare, especially now that she was helping out at the condiments stand, where Mrs Troyer roped her in to help her sell her jams and honey.

But even so, the occasional shy smile from John now and again, did not go unnoticed. There was definitely something brewing there, and it was only a matter of time before something extraordinary hatched. Then again, Nikki's romantic side often blinded her to the harsh realities of life. It's just that here in this community everything was so real and so transparent.

"If you stare any longer, you'll set that stall on fire." A deep timber voice spoke beside her.

Ripped out of her reverie, she cleared her throat and scrambled for a tea towel.

"I'm sorry, my mind was elsewhere, how may help you?" she said plastering a smile on her face at the man standing in front of her.

"The name's Abraham," he said with a wide grin.

"Pardon?" she asked confused.

"You're Nikki right, Eva's niece?"

Get it together, she reprimanded herself and shifted her weight. "Um... yes, I'm Nikki," she said half embarrassed. "Can I interest you in any of Mrs Troyer's jams?"

He laughed and shook his head, then pointed to the honey-nut-brittle snacks. It was then that she noticed the young boy standing next to him.

"Oh I see," she grinned and looked over the edge of the table at the blonde haired boy, "You have a sweet tooth don't you?

The boy nodded, with his thumb stuck in his mouth and Nikki handed Abraham a jar of candy.

"He fancy's you."

Nikki's hand froze and clutched the jar of candy tighter. "I'm sorry?"

"John. He lost his wife three years ago, I thought he'd never move on, but I can see he fancy's you."

Nikki felt a blush creep to her cheeks, and she fumbled with her apron, averting her gaze every which way. "I'm sure you're imagining things," she muttered under her breath.

"I see the obvious. You like him too *jah*?"

Nikki's eyes grew wide, was it that obvious to the surrounding people? She dared to glance past him, half expecting John to be looking her way, but he was busy with a customer.

"He's a fine gentleman, but I'm not sure about your assumptions."

Abraham didn't utter another word, simply smiled and tipped his hat before walking off with his son. Nikki's heart was beating a million miles a second. She had only spoken to John a few times; it was hardly ground for a relationship of any sorts. And worst of all, now it was even harder to keep her eyes off John. Her curiosity to see if Abraham was indeed right, overrode her sanity. And by the end of the day, she had spent every ounce of control to keep herself from staring at him all day. Needless to say, she hastily packed up the stall and rushed home, just to get away from the heated tension that was so obviously brewing between them, and worst of all, they didn't have to say a single word.

John had to do everything in his power to stay true to Mary, although she had been dead for over three years, he couldn't deny the obvious attraction he felt towards this new girl. And he had noticed just after Abraham's visit to her stall, she had grown overly clumsy, but also noticed that she kept looking his way. Abraham was the one who told him that Nikki fancied him, and at first he didn't want to believe him. What would a beautiful Englischer who wrote fantasy novels for a living want to do with a boring Amish man? He had done his homework on her, and with the help of Eva, he had found out all he needed to know about her. And even though a union between him and the Englischer was out of the question and practically impossible, he could not deny the feelings he had started to develop for her.

This afternoon however, unlike other afternoons, Nikki had rushed to get home and John couldn't help but wonder if it was too presumptuous of him to think that she fancied him. Maybe he misinterpreted her occasional smile in his direction, and all it was, was curiosity.

"John dear," Eva said when she came walking along the path towards his stall where he had already packed all his produce away in crates.

"Eva, it's rather late for you, shouldn't you be home?"

The old woman smiled and held out her hand. "I can be wherever I want to be at whatever time," she said stubbornly.

"That is true, so how can I help you?"

Eva blushed and shrugged. "Well you see, I'll be staying over at Gretchen's place tonight to help with the baby, her daughter has finally gone into labour, so I was wondering if you could go by the house and just let Nikki know."

Surprised, John cocked a brow. He sniffed a plot brewing here, but he nodded anyway. "Of course, when can she expect you back?"

"Who knows, babies come when they want, we can only wait."

He laughed and stacked the last of his crates on top of the others. "I'll let her know," he agreed with a smile.

Eva turned to leave and then stopped, "Oh and maybe you can take her some dinner, I haven't cooked, and these city girls don't have the foggiest on what to do in a kitchen."

If ever there was a clever plot, he thought amused, but even then he felt the small flutter of butterflies deep down in the pit of his stomach.

Chapter 6

Nikki looked up at the cuckoo clock against the wall. Aunt Eva was never this late, and she was starting to get worried and frustrated. She had no idea where to even start looking if she had to go find her aunt. She paced the living room impatiently and kept looking out the window, but there was no sight of her aunt.

Irritated, Nikki went to the kitchen, opening cupboard to find some food to start cooking. Other than vegetables, there wasn't much else. In the pantry she found some beans and eggs. How on earth Aunt Eva managed to always cook such delicious dinners with so little at her disposal, was beyond her, she thought as she flopped down on one of the chairs in the kitchen? Just then someone knocked on the door and she didn't think twice to go and open it, only to be shocked to find John standing there with a dish in his hand.

"Good evening," he said politely and shrugged holding up the dish. "I come bearing gifts."

Nikki gaped at him at first before she realized, she looked like a complete idiot.

"Do come in," she said and stepped aside. "I have no idea where Aunt Eva is, but you can put it in the kitchen."

"Eva is over at Gretchen's house, her daughter is having her baby and she's helping the midwife."

Nikki closed the door behind her but didn't dare move, simply watched John disappear into the kitchen before she finally followed. When she entered the kitchen he had already taken out two plates and two glasses.

"She sent me to bring you some food, and let you know she would be home very late, if at all."

Being alone in a house with John made her feel giddy and watching him move about the kitchen as if he belonged there was even more intriguing. The men she knew back home were complete brute's who cared about nothing but themselves.

"Your aunt told me you write novels," he said casually.

So they've been talking about her, she thought and a kaleidoscope of butterflies fluttered about in her stomach. "Well sort of, but I haven't touched anything since the first day I ran into you."

John stopped mid dishing up food and looked at her. "Why have you stopped?"

Nikki pulled herself together and took the salt and pepper shaker and put it on the table. "For one, electricity is a problem, and a laptop relies on that. Secondly, I'm waiting for a new contract, but I've grown tired of the type of novels I'm expected to write."

He continued dishing up food and then pulled out her chair for her. "And what do you want to write?"

She shrugged as she sat down. "I don't quite know to be honest; I just need some inspiration I guess."

"I see, well I'm sure you'll find inspiration once you're back in the city."

Before she could reply, John bowed his head and said grace. She was too consumed by him to bow her head, and when he said Amen and looked up at her, it was almost as if time went into a suspended state. It was John who severed the current between them when he finally looked away and reached for the salt.

"It's cottage pie. Eva said you like it."

Completely unnerved by the moment they shared earlier, she fumbled with her fork and nodded. "I do, and it's also the only thing I can make."

"You can't cook?"

She blushed and looked down at her plate. "I lived off microwave dinners and very basic meals like, instant noodles, scrambled eggs and toast."

John chuckled and her stomach tumbled wildly. The rest of the evening they spent talking about her life in the city. How she became a writer and what had driven her to come to River Stone. John told her about his wife and how hard it had been for him to finally let her go. But somewhere in between she realized that she wasn't only falling in love with life in River Stone, and its simple but practical ways, she had started to develop feelings for John.

By around eight that evening and after they shared a cup of tea, John finally got up and helped her to clear the dishes.

"Tell me something," she started nervously.

"What do you want to know?"

"Is it a sin for a man and woman who aren't, you know, together, to be alone in a house?"

The amused look on John's face made her smile, and when he laughed, she laughed.

"We're not sixteen anymore. Things are different for widows and adults in the Amish community. Why do you ask?"

Nikki blushed profusely and turned away to hide her face from him, and as casually as she could she said, "I was just wondering in general, that's all."

She felt him standing close behind her and she a shiver of anticipation ran down her spine.

"Is that really all, or are you willing to admit there's something going on between us?"

With that she spun around and gasped, "That's absolutely ludicrous! We're complete opposites."

The moment the words were out, she regretted them, but when John didn't react shocked or hurt by her words, she took a deep steadying breath. "What I mean is that we're two completely different individuals. Whatever is going on between us, is... is, actually I have no idea what it is."

John folded the dish towel and set it down on the sink before turning to her. "To be honest, I don't know either, but I'm not one to ignore the obvious. My father used to tell me, if something feels right, and there is no sin to be committed, then it's the path you are destined to follow."

Nikki was speechless, but instead of going after him, she let him go.

"What on earth just happened?" she said loudly as she pressed the heels of her palms against her eyes.

Chapter 7

A week had passed and John had been busy on his own farm making sure everything was ready. The shed he had promised to build Mary was finally finished, and all that was left to do was furnishing it. It was a small little building made out of wood, with a thatched roof, something he hadn't done before, but it worked out well. The front of the shed had a large open window that overlooked the creek down below, and the scenery was something out of this world. He always loved nature and having this piece of land was perfect for him. When he and Mary had gotten married, they had such high hopes to have a family, but she could not bear any children. Even then, he was happy to grow old with the love of his life and have nieces and nephews visit the farm instead. But since then things have changed, although he thought fondly of Mary, he no longer felt lost and bereft. It was a chapter in his life that had come to an end and the time had come for him to move on to the next chapter.

He arrived in River Stone shortly after ten on the Sunday morning. Everyone was still at the church service, which he had missed due to a detour he had taken, but it was worth his while. He headed straight to Eva's house to wait for them to return from church.

Not long after, the two women came strolling up the path towards the house. From where he stood, he could see the smile on Eva's face and in turn the uncertainty on Nikki's.

"John, what a lovely surprise dear boy, what brings you to River Stone on a Sunday?" Eva said when they drew closer.

John smiled and greeted Eva and then looked at Nikki.

"I'm actually here to see Nikki, can you give us a moment?" he asked, never taking his eyes off of her.

"I'm sure we can all get a cup of tea inside," Nikki protested.

Eva laughed, "Nicole, why don't you go with John and I'll get the tea ready."

John simply smiled at her and he could see the nervousness in her eyes.

Nikki felt her heart do a gazillion leaps as she stood facing John. After their whole debacle in the kitchen a week ago, all she could think about was him. She hashed out every possible reason why they could never be together, but each time her heart ached, knowing she would be losing more than a chance at happiness. She was a writer, not a house wife or a cook. She wasn't like any of the other women in the Amish community, and that was exactly what John needed, a good Amish wife that could cook and sew.

"What do you want?" she blurted out abruptly.

John looked at her and smiled and that was another thing that frustrated her. No matter how rude she was or how direct she tried to be, he seemed oblivious to her intensions.

"I want to show you something," he said quietly, "But you'll have to come for a ride with me."

"A ride where?"

"To my farm, out at Trumbull, it's a few miles north."

Confused she looked back at the house, "But Aunt Eva is making tea."

"That's fine, we can have tea, but I would really like you to come with me, I promise to bring you back home."

She should have said no, but she couldn't, and an hour later, she was sitting next to John in his buggy heading to his farm. The ride to Trumbull was pleasant, but she could hardly breathe at the rate her heart was beating in her chest. All along the way John introduced her to the farms along the road side, giving her some insight on every family who lived there and shared some historical facts about the area.

He finally turned into a narrow road, and up ahead, the farmhouse stood on the hill. It looked like it had always been a part of the pale green hills that surrounded it. A beautiful white wooden house, box shaped with a blue door dead centre. There were square windows on either side of the house with matching blue shutters flung open invitingly. The path that leads to the house was made of stone and snaked up from the small gate to the front door. It was nothing short of magnificent in its own peculiar way. Almost instantly, Nikki had a plot for a novel brewing in her mind. Being here in Trumbull at John's farm had awakened her creativity again, but this time it had nothing to do with dragons and fairies.

"Here we are," he said drawing her back to reality.

"This is your house?" she asked awestruck.

"Yes, but I'll show the house in a bit, I want to show you something else."

A flutter of excitement swirled up inside of her as she followed him around the back of the house to a small shed that stood a few feet away from the main house. Past the shed was a small patch of trees that lead down into a creek. It was a complete sensory overload.

"This way," he said and took her around to the entrance.

"I'm not sure why you brought me here," she finally admitted.

"I wanted to show you were I live, wait here and have a look around."

Without a word he disappeared, leaving her in the small cabin. In front of the large window was a desk. To her right a book shelf, with a few books. Against the one wall were two matching chairs, with floral printed cushions and a small table between them.

It was a cosy little nook where a person could simply hide away from reality, she thought as she took it all in. What was even more beautiful was the view. The hills sloped down from the mountain and dove into the creek not too far from the small cabin and from where she stood she could hear the rushing water down below.

John appeared a few minutes later and placed a box on the desk. "I found this, and I thought you might like it."

A small frown formed between her brows as she looked down at the box and she bit her lip. She had no idea what John had gotten her, but whatever it was, it belonged in this cabin, and that can only mean one thing. The though alone had her mind spinning.

He opened the box and then pulled out a vintage Olivetti typewriter and her heart melted.

"You got me a type writer?" she asked in shock.

He smiled and placed it in the centre of the desk. "I did, the thing is, I want you to write, it's who you are. I don't expect you to be a domesticated housewife. There is no denying that I'm in love with you. Every day I wake up and all I see is you and I figured if you can come here, write to your hearts content, I can make you happy."

Nikki's eyes shot full of tears, and she clasped her hands in front her mouth. She was officially speechless.

"If you don't want me I'll understand," John said and this time she could see he was also nervous.

She walked towards the type writer and ran her fingers over the bubble keys that sloped upwards. If anything she would have given up writing if it meant being with John. But now, this gesture on its own had proven to her that he was willing to accept her regardless so their differences.

She slowly turned to him and smiled, tears glimmering in her eyes. "I didn't think you would approve of the fact that I'm a writer, or of the fact that I have no idea how to cook anything other than Cottage Pie."

John laughed and reached for her hands and brought them to his lips. "I can teach you how to cook, if you teach me how to use a type writer."

Nikki laughed and cried all at once, and John pulled her into his arms. "Yes," she whispered, and John gently kissed her tears from her cheeks.

"I have a generator, so you can bring your laptop too."

With that Nikki flung her arms around his neck and clung to him. So overwhelmed with emotion that she wasn't sure if she would ever recover, she pressed her lips against his.

~*~

"Cloe is such a darling name," Aunt Eva said as she bounced the little dark haired girl on her lap, "But it's not really that Amish."

Nikki laughed and brought the spoon full of baby food to her little girl's mouth. "John named her, if anything it's as Amish as it will ever get."

The trio sat in the meadow outside of the cabin while Nikki fed Cloe, Aunt Eva sat holding the precious little girl on her lap and John worked on building the tree house for his little girl to play on.

"Do you think she'll like it?" he called from the first treehouse.

"She'll love it!" Nikki called and smiled at her husband.

Just over a year ago, she would never have through herself to be a wife, much less a mother, but in a blink of an eye all of that had changed. With John's help she managed to publish her very first book on 'Becoming Amish'. It was their story, of how relentless love can overcome any diversity between two people who are destined to be together.

Ruth 1:16-17

16 But Ruth replied, "Don't urge me to leave you or to turn back from you. Where you go I will go, and where you stay I will stay. Your people will be my people and your God my God. 17 Where you die I will die, and there I will be buried. May the Lord deal with me, be it ever so severely, if even death separates you and me."

MAMMI

There was a slight buzzing in her ears but it had been there for the better part of two weeks, something Rachel had grown accustomed to hearing. She knew it wasn't medical but it alarmed her all the same.

It does not take a doctor to see I am blocking outside noise in my own way, she thought ruefully.

It wasn't until Joanna tugged gently on her skirt that she realized someone was trying to get her attention.

"*Mammi*? Bishop Bachman is summoning you."

Rachel glanced down at her small daughter and offered her a quick smile.

"Oh."

She looked toward where Joanna pointed and indeed, the Bishop was waving almost comically for her to join him.

"Come along, *liebchen*," she said to the six-year-old and Joanna followed closely on her mother's heels.

"Lovely service, Bishop," Rachel told the elder without preamble. She did not want to give him a chance to open with platitudes.

He nodded appreciatively and patted Joanna on the head endearingly.

"Did you enjoy it also, little Jo?"

Rachel cringed inwardly, hoping her outspoken child would have something nice to say and to her relief, Joanna nodded eagerly.

"Yes, Bishop Bachman. I like listening to you speak about forgiveness and repentance."

Rachel exhaled slowly, hardly realizing she had been holding her breath.

"They are lessons which we must never forget, regardless of how difficult a time we encounter, right Jo?"

"Yes, Bishop," the child agreed and Rachel tried to ignore the obvious message the Bishop had delivered to her specifically.

"Very good, Jo. Off you go then. I would like to speak with your mother alone."

Rachel stifled a groan. She had intentionally brought Joanna along in hopes that she would not be left to hear the bishop's words of wisdom that afternoon.

"Walk along side me, Rachel," the Bishop ordered and Rachel idly wondered what would happen if she politely refused. It was a fleeting thought, a wicked fantasy rather than something she was apt to do.

She loved Bishop Bachman well. He was a decent man and strong leader. That did not mean she wished to be subjected to his well-meaning advice.

"Of course," she agreed and they headed away from the congregation toward the pond in the middle of the Troyer farm.

"How are you faring these days, Rachel?"

She inadvertently gritted her teeth together and the bishop seemed to catch her expression before she could hide it.

"Rachel, I know this is a trying time for you but I want you to understand you are not alone."

She nodded, trying to force a cheerful smile onto her face but she was certain she was about to dissolve into a puddle of tears if he continued to press her.

"I know," she replied. "I am blessed to have the support of my family and the district."

Bishop Bachman stopped walking and turned to regard her.

"And the Umbels?"

The familiar lump formed quickly, barely giving Rachel enough time to swallow her misery.

She shook her head.

"I do not see much of them but in casual passing," she confessed. The bishop sighed regretfully, his eyes moving toward her in-laws who tried not to stare back at them in the distance. Bishop Bachman returned his gaze to Rachel.

"That is unfortunate but you must understand they feel as badly as you do. It will take time to heal but everyone will get there, *Gotte* willing."

Rachel did not answer, her own eyes shifting back toward where her daughter tagged along after some older children. She purposely avoided looking at the Umbels.

"You already know that your focus must be on Joanna and she seems to be thriving despite the circumstances."

Rachel nodded, her fingers reaching up to play with a strand of honey-blonde hair. It was a nervous habit she had forsaken years earlier but it seemed to have resurfaced in the past weeks.

"Who is helping you on the farm?"

Rachel wondered why he asked questions he already knew the answer to but she dared not voice her own inquiry.

He does not mean any harm. You must not lose your temper with the Bishop.

"I am faring just fine," she fibbed, returning her stare to his concerned eyes. She forced a tight smile onto her lips.

"It is not a big farm, Bishop and I really do not need much to keep it going. Most of my income is from my quilts these days. The farm is secondary."

"Be that as it may, Rachel, you should not be tending to it alone. I will see about having someone help you."

She opened her mouth to protest.

The last thing she wanted was another neighbor prying into the intimate and embarrassing details of what had happened with Eli.

It is not as if they do not already know. They likely knew before I did, she thought bitterly. All Rachel wanted to do was disappear into a world with her daughter and forget the rest of the community.

Overnight it seemed, the life she had cherished in the close-knit Amish district had become a place of alienation and isolation.

The people she had once wanted to share her life with became those to avoid.

"Rachel?" the Bishop pressed. "Will you allow me to find you help?"

She knew there would be no point in arguing with the man. His intentions were good and she knew his worry was genuine.

"That will be fine," she replied. "I should get back to Joanna."

He nodded although Rachel could tell he did not consider the conversation finished.

It is not the last I have heard of this, she thought, sighing silently. *I wonder if I will ever hear the last of this.*

"Hello."

Samuel looked up from the fence post and did a double take as he saw the man standing a few feet away.

"Hello," Samuel replied, rising to his full height. He dropped the hammer in his tool belt and cocked his head to the side, peering at the stranger. He brushed a strand of light brown hair from his face and stared inquisitively at the man.

"Do you work for hire or are you employed by this farmer?"

Samuel's brown eyes narrowed suspiciously.

"I would ask if you were from the IRS but something tells me you aren't," he replied, a slightly sarcastic tone lacing his words.

The stranger chuckled and extended a hand.

"No, you would be correct. I am not from the IRS. My name is Mark Bachman. I am a Bishop with the Amish district just that way. You are?"

Samuel eyed his outstretched palm reluctantly but stepped forward to accept it.

"Samuel Baker."

"Good to meet you, Mr. Baker. I have a member of our district who needs some help on her farm. She has the unfortunate task of tending the land herself, something that happened quite recently. Is this something which might interest you?"

Samuel withdrew his hand and stepped back, his brow knitting in consternation.

"Don't you people help your own?" he asked gruffly. The Bishop seemed amused by his question.

"We try to," he replied. "But sometimes we need outsider assistance. Of course, you would be compensated well for your efforts."

Samuel looked around, wiping the sweat from his neck. He stared at the Bishop, considering the man's words.

Work had been sparse and he had bills to pay. Samuel knew he would be foolish to turn down an offer like that but he could not help but feel suspicious of this bizarre chance encounter.

"How did you come across me?" Samuel demanded. Bishop Bachman pointed at his wagon just down the dirt road.

"I happened to be driving by and I saw you. I have just finished services and I am returning to my home. Truth be told, I think you were a sign from God. I was going to begin looking for help for Rachel in the morning but here you are, working on a Sunday."

Samuel nodded slowly.

"Unfortunately, my bills don't understand days of the week," he muttered and the elder laughed aloud.

"It is one of the many trials and tribulations the English face, I fear. If you were to accept my proposal, you would have Sundays as a day of rest."

Samuel tried to remember a time when any day had been a day of rest.

I haven't rested in years.

So what do you say? Would you be willing to help Rachel on her farm?"

"Is it steady work?"

Samuel wondered why he bothered voicing the question; he was already going to take the job, steady work or not.

"Yes, it is," Bishop Bachman replied. "My guess is for as long as you're willing to do it."

Samuel nodded.

"When does it start?"

"You can begin tomorrow if you are available."

Sam grinned for the first time since meeting the Amish man and extended his palm again.

"I'm available."

"*Mammi*, where did *Daed* go?"

It was not the first time which Joanna had asked the question but it never ceased to send a thousand needles into Rachel's heart.

"Joanna, what have I told you about your father?" she replied, grinding her jaw.

"He has gone away," the child chirped. "But where? And when will he return?"

"He is not coming back!" Rachel's voice was much harsher than she had intended and a look of hurt crossed over her face.

"I am sorry, *Mammi*," she whispered and Rachel was instantly filled with shame.

She is only a child, longing for her father! You have no cause to snap at her like that!

Rachel extended her arms.

"No, *liebchen*, I am sorry," she gasped, tears springing to her green eyes. "Come here."

Dutifully, Joanna ran into her mother's arms and the two embraced.

"*Daed* is not coming back, not ever," she breathed. "I am sorry to tell you that but you must stop asking about him."

"Why *Mammi*? Why can I not ask about him?"

Rachel bit on her lower lip and buried her face in Joanna's soft blonde mop of hair.

"You must go now, Jo. You will be late for school."

They parted and Jo looked up at her mother.

"Why are you crying, *Mammi*?"

"I only have something in my eye," she fibbed. "Off you go now."

Begrudgingly, Joanna trudged toward the door, glancing back at her mother one last time. Rachel waved encouragingly and painted a smile upon her face.

She is too young to understand any of this. How can I explain it when I barely understand myself.

Rachel sighed and turned back to the sink where she was doing the breakfast dishes.

She had a mountain of work to accomplish that day and she did not know if she would get half of it done. She recalled her conversation with Bishop Bachman the previous day.

I shouldn't be so head strong. I do need help and I should get some assistance before I lose control of the farm. It has only been two weeks and things are already becoming overwhelming.

Rachel reluctantly realized she would be forced to ask her family for help but she knew with their help came an earful of unsolicited advice.

A knock at the front door shattered her thoughts and she glanced back to see Bishop Bachman on the porch.

She waved him inside, drying her hands on her apron.

Ah, speaking of unsolicited advice...

She was immediately filled with contrition.

You should be grateful he cares enough about you to see if you are well.

"*Guder mariye*, Rachel," he called as he entered the small house.

"*Guder mariye*," she replied. "To what do I owe the pleasure, Bishop?"

She hoped he was not about to speak to her about Eli again.

"I have someone whom I would like you to meet," he said as she moved to join him at the entranceway.

Rachel's eyebrows shot up to her hairline.

He cannot mean...

Instantly, Bishop Bachman seemed to read the look of dread on her face.

"It is a handyman," he said quickly and Rachel was filled with a relief so strong, it almost knocked her to her knees.

Of course he would not bring a suitor to my door so soon. Why am I looking at everyone like an enemy?

"Already you have found a handyman?" she replied, surprised. "You must have had someone in mind."

They moved toward the door and the Bishop shook his head.

"No, actually I chanced upon him on the way home yesterday."

As they stepped onto the veranda, Rachel started in shock.

"Rachel Umbel, this is Samuel Baker."

Rachel recovered from her initial reaction immediately stuck her hand out.

"Ah, thank you for coming to my assistance, Mr. Baker," she said quickly, shifting her eyes away from his face.

"No problem," he replied gruffly and Rachel wondered if he had noticed her reaction. They shook hands quickly.

"Tell me where you want me to go," he said without hesitation and Rachel could sense he was not the conversational type. She found the realization heartwarming.

I will not be forced to entertain him or answer questions all day long, she thought with some happiness.

"Do you have any experience in working with animals? The horses need grooming."

Samuel nodded and looked around, spotting the barn.

Without another word, he disappeared toward the stables, leaving the Bishop and Rachel alone.

"Who is he?" Rachel asked when he was out of earshot. "I have never seen him around the district before."

"As I said, I only just chanced upon him yesterday."

Rachel gnawed on her lower lip, debating whether to ask the obvious question or not.

"What happened to his face?" she finally whispered, her curiosity winning out. The Bishop shrugged.

"I did not think to ask," he replied nonchalantly, turning to leave. "I will be back to pick him up at four o'clock."

Rachel nodded, watching at the Bishop got onto his wagon.

He did not think to ask how that man's face got so horribly disfigured? She thought, shaking her head. *How could he not wish to know?*

Rachel forced the thought of Samuel from her mind and began addressing her long list of chores.

She had her own issues to worry about without bringing in an Englisher's problems also.

Maybe it is time to go back to the city, he thought. *Work is too scarce in Amish country and even if this is steady income, I don't belong here.*

Samuel wondered if he belonged anywhere anymore.

It had been five years since he had called any place "home", wandering from town to town like a nomad. He had no friends, no ties and no money.

At least I will have a better shot of employment in Detroit.

Branch County had been kind to him given his appearance but the thought of returning to the city filled him with a sick which never truly left him.

There was too great a chance he would see Holly in Detroit, no matter where he went.

Detroit has a population of third quarters of a million people. You will not see Holly.

He tried to shove the thought of her from his mind but it seemed her anguished face would forever be etched there.

Maybe in another year, he thought, blinking quickly against his burning lids. *Maybe then I will be able to return to Detroit and face what I have done.*

But he didn't believe himself. It was the same thing he told himself every year around the time of the anniversary.

Sam knew that the pain did not go away, no matter how much he avoided contact with others or hid himself away in the boonies.

It wouldn't happen next near.

He would never go home because home did not exist for him anymore.

The late afternoon sun filtered into the front room and Rachel glanced up suddenly, blinking. She peered down at the quilt she had been sewing and then at the clock in the corner of the room.

How long have I been in here? She thought in shock. She had worked through lunch and her fingers were throbbing.

She had wanted to finish the piece for sale at market on Friday but she had not meant to spend a great deal of time on it, not when there was so much else to be done before Joanna returned from school.

She rose from the rocking chair and peered out the window into the front yard.

And what happened to the Englisher?

A spark of anger coursed through her as she threw open the front door, slightly blinded by the rays. She had not seen him since first thing that morning when she had sent him to groom the horses.

He is probably taking a nap. Why did I agree to let the Bishop bring someone here?

Angrily, she hurried around the back of the house toward the barn and threw open the doors, freezing in her tracks.

The two horses were gleaming and well-groomed in spotless stalls with fresh hay. Samuel had swept out the interior and maintained the unoccupied booths also.

Rachel was sure she had never seen the stables so clean.

She was immediately ashamed for thinking the worst of the Englisher and she looked around to see where he had gone.

If he is napping, he has certainly earned a rest, she thought wryly. *This is more than Eli could accomplish in a day.*

She found Samuel in the garden, weeding through the tomato plants, sweat glistening on his neck and shoulders. There was no sweat on his scarred face and Rachel wondered if he was in constant pain. She certainly hoped not.

She watched him for a moment, touched by his work ethic. No one had guided him to the garden; he had simply taken the task upon himself as he had cleaning out the barn.

"You did good work with the horses," she called out to him. He barely raised his head but he nodded slightly to acknowledge her words.

"Have you taken any water or eaten yet?"

Samuel paused and glanced at her for a moment, seeming unsure of himself. Rachel was struck at how bright brown his eyes seemed through his mangled face and yet she did not find looking at him as unsettling as she had earlier.

Despite his exterior, Rachel could sense a gentleness beneath him, one he seemed to want to keep hidden.

"No, I am fine," he finally answered, turning back to the plants.

"I cannot have you fainting in the sun," Rachel insisted sternly. "Please come in the house for some water at least."

He paused and Rachel reasoned his thirst must have won out in the end.

"All right," he agreed but Rachel thought she heard a slight resentment in his tone.

Silently, he followed her back toward the house and into the side door.

In the kitchen, they didn't speak as Rachel fixed him a glass of lemonade. As she placed the glass before him, she thought he was about to protest but he shut his mouth and took a long sip.

Rachel turned back to the refrigerator.

"I will fix us some lunch," she announced.

"No thank you," Samuel answered quickly. "I should get back to work."

She glanced at him over her shoulder and shook her head.

"You have accomplished more today than I had expected to do all week," she replied. "You can take time for lunch."

Samuel was silent but she could feel him watching her as she made a plate of cheese, bread and fruit.

She set the plate at the table and joined him.

"Do you believe in God?" she asked, glancing at him as he reached for his food. He seemed taken aback by the question.

"I used to," he replied, ripping off a hunk of bread with surprisingly straight teeth. "But he doesn't seem to come around much for me these days."

Rachel nodded and bowed her head.

"Thank you, *Gotte* for sending me help when I needed it most. Please bless our food. Amen."

Samuel dropped his bread and looked embarrassed.

"Amen," he echoed quickly. "I'm sorry. It didn't occur to me to pray."

Rachel smiled and began to eat.

"There is no need to apologize. You are entitled to your beliefs. I did not wish to exclude you if you wished to join," she explained.

Samuel chewed on his morsels slowly, studying her furtively and Rachel sensed that he wanted to say something.

You invited him in to eat. You should encourage him to speak, she thought but in truth, she was rather enjoying the silence of someone who knew nothing about her or her past.

"Did your husband die recently?"

The question was blunt and caught Rachel off guard. She stared at him with clear green eyes, her mouth slightly agape.

Her first instinct was indignation but suddenly, she began to laugh.

"In a way," she replied and Samuel stared at her, his brow raised in surprise at her odd reaction. He did not question her further.

"I am sorry for your loss," he muttered, fixating his eyes on the table. "It is not easy to lose someone you love."

Rachel was moved by his tone and despite her resolve not to engage in conversation, she found herself intrigued by the hardworking stranger.

"Are you married?" she asked.

"Not anymore."

He is as vague as I am, she thought, partly amused, partly annoyed. She wondered if he was simply treating her the way she was treating him.

Do unto others...

"You are very good around the farm," she told him. "Do you have a farm of your own?"

He shook his head.

"No," he replied. "I grew up on one though, before I moved to Michigan."

The sound of hooves approaching the house caused them to glance out of the window and suddenly Rachel saw Joanna skip around the side of the property.

"My daughter is home," she said, rising and dusting the crumbs from her apron as Joanna came slipping through the door. "But I can't see who has come by wagon."

"*Mammi*, Bishop Bachman is - "

Joanna turned to stone as she took in the stranger in her kitchen. Her small face became a mask of fear as she stared at Samuel, her mouth open with fear.

Terrified that Joanna would say something impolite, Rachel piped up immediately.

"Joanna, this is Mr. Baker. He will be helping us on the farm. Samuel, this is my daughter Joanna."

She nudged her daughter gently but Joanna could not seem to overcome her horror of Samuel's scarred face and hid her eyes in her mother's skirt.

Rachel turned apologetically to Samuel.

"I am sorry," she started. "She's shy – "

It was at that moment that she realized Samuel's face was a statue still as Joanna's had been. He gaped at the girl, his fierce eyes wide with an emotion Rachel could not place.

"Samuel, are you all right?" Rachel asked.

"Hello? Rachel? Are you here?" Bishop Bachman called, entering the house through the front door. The elder's voice seemed to shatter Samuel's trance-like state.

"I didn't know you had a daughter," Samuel mumbled, spinning to leave. "I – I'm sorry. I can't come back here."

He disappeared from the kitchen, almost barreling over Bishop Bachman who appeared in the doorway. The bishop's smile faded as he watched Samuel run out the door toward his wagon.

"What happened? Did it go badly today?" he demanded but Rachel had no answer for him.

She pulled Joanna close to her, her heart racing.

"*Mammi,* is that man a monster?" Joanna whispered.

"Dear *Gotte*, I hope not, *liebchen*," Rachel murmured in response.

The fire raged hot and terrifying. Joanna's screams could scarcely be heard above the popping of the wood beams and Rachel raced about looking for her daughter.

"Joanna!" she cried, tears streaking down her face. "Joanna, where are you?"

But the child only continued to shriek and Rachel tried to find her despite the billowing, blinding smoke encasing the barn.

She saw a movement out of the corner of her eye and suddenly, Samuel emerged, holding Joanna, limp in his arms, his eyes wild.

Rachel began to howl.

Rachel started awake, her body drenched in sweat.

Without hesitation, she slipped from her bed and rushed into Joanna's room, pushing open the door in fear.

The child lay sleeping peacefully, her body half curled with a soft smile on her face.

Slowly, Rachel's breath steadied but she could not bring herself to leave the room and she slid quietly onto the single mattress beside her daughter.

She could not forget the crazed expression in Samuel's eyes from her dream.

Who did I allow into my house? She thought, willing herself to be calm.

It did not matter; he would not be back.

For some inexplicable reason, the reality of that filled Rachel with sadness.

As dawn broke, Rachel had not slept again and reluctantly she left Joanna's side to make breakfast.

There was a darkness to the day and Rachel sensed they were in for rain.

It will be a good day to work on my quilts, she thought and immediately she was grateful for the work that Samuel had done on the farm the previous day. Losing a day to bad weather was something she could not afford in her position.

Confusion filled her.

How can I be thankful he helped and fear him also?

She was beginning to wonder if the dream had not been a warning but something else.

It is irrelevant now. Samuel is gone and you must find someone else to help on the farm.

Sighing, she continued to fix the morning meal and Joanna eventually slipped downstairs.

"*Guder mariye, Mammi,*" the child chirped, slipping onto a chair.

"Hello, *liebchen.* Did you sleep well?"

Joanna nodded.

"I had a wonderful dream," she told her mother, her bright green eyes wide.

"What did you dream of?"

"The Englisher from yesterday," she replied and Rachel stared at her in shock.

"What of him?" she demanded, her face growing hot with worry.

"He brought me to a field with flowers, all with many colors and tall grasses. There was another little girl there too. He told me her name was Brittany. She and I skipped and played, picking flowers and praying together. And you know what *Mammi*?"

Unexpected tears filled Rachel's eyes.

"What, Jo?"

"The Englisher's face was not scarred. He was pleasant to look at."

Rachel's voice caught in her throat.

We both dreamt of him last night but very different dreams. I wonder what it means.

"Eat your breakfast, *liebchen.*"

Joanna nodded agreeably, leaving Joanna to her thoughts.

Samuel lay on his bed, unable to move as memories consumed him, filling him with devastation and pain.

I reacted very badly yesterday, he thought, his heart heavy but he could not bring himself to move. *I will never be able to overcome this. I will be haunted by Brittany and Holly until I die.*

Seeing Joanna Umbel had stirred something in him which he had tried to supress for years but he should have known it would rear its ugly head at the most inopportune time.

Now I have alarmed Rachel and ruined the only chance I have had for steady employment in such a long time.

There was more to it, something Samuel did not want to admit to himself.

He was strangely drawn to Rachel, despite her somewhat standoffish nature.

Maybe that is why I am drawn to her, he reasoned. *She is not pushy or intrusive. She leaves me alone but she seems caring. I wonder what happened to her husband.*

There was a knock on the door to his basement apartment and Samuel made no move to answer it.

"Samuel? It's Bishop Bachman."

Sam groaned inwardly, cursing himself for allowing the bishop to know where he lived.

"Bishop, I thought I told you I'm not going back to the Umbel farm," he yelled from his spot on his cot.

"Yes, but I would like to speak with you for a moment. Please, Samuel, it's raining outside."

Sam rolled his eyes but reluctantly rose to let the older man inside.

It wasn't very godly to leave him standing in the water after all.

"Come in," he muttered begrudgingly, stepping aside for Bishop Bachman to enter. The elder removed his hat, droplets of water falling to the entranceway. He looked at Samuel apologetically.

"I am sorry to bother you so early, Samuel but I wanted to stop by and see if you had changed your mind."

Sam shook his head quickly.

"No," he replied flatly. "But thanks for checking in."

"May I ask what happened?"

Sam peered at him questioningly.

"Are you people always like this?"

The bishop seemed genuinely tickled even though Samuel had meant to sound gruff.

"If you mean do we always take care of one another then the answer is yes."

A foreign pang of appreciation sparked through Sam as he stared at the man.

"I am going to be frank with you, Samuel. Rachel is going through a very difficult time. Her husband shamed her family and the community by leaving with another woman. He has been shunned and it is not something that we take lightly. Unfortunately, Rachel has found herself feeling isolated also. She does not wish to seek counsel and I cannot say that I am surprised she has retreated into herself. I have grown concerned for her."

Samuel was shocked by the revelation.

What kind of idiot leaves a woman like that? He thought angrily. His mind went to Joanna and he swallowed a lump in his throat.

What kind of man leaves behind a beautiful daughter when he is so blessed to have one?

"When I saw you working the other day, I got the impression that you, too, enjoy your solitude. Am I mistaken?" Bishop Bachman continued.

Sam chuckled somewhat mirthlessly.

"As a rule, yes," he replied. The bishop nodded understandingly.

"I felt that your presence might be beneficial to Rachel, both from a work standpoint but also as a silent support to her. Honestly, I am surprised that you two did not get along better."

Samuel did not respond but suddenly the Bishop's unexpected approach made sense.

He saw a damaged man and he matched me with a damaged woman.

Samuel was unsure how to feel about it.

"I will not keep you, Samuel but if you should happen to change your mind, I am certain that Rachel could still use the assistance...and the companionship."

Bishop Bachman turned to leave.

"Wait a minute," Sam called after him. "I thought you Amish didn't like outsiders."

The older man turned to smile enigmatically.

"Perhaps you will not always be an outsider, Samuel. Perhaps there is a place for you in this world with us."

The idea was stunning and he watched the Bishop replace his hat, disappearing into the rain.

Did he just suggest that I join the Amish? That is crazy.

But long after Bishop Bachman left, Samuel could not shake the spark of hope which had been ignited in his belly.

How long had it been since he belonged somewhere?

The buzzing in her ears was louder than usual that morning and it did not seem to lessen no matter how Rachel tried to distract herself.

Suddenly, it seemed accompanied by a roar and her heart racing, she wondered if there was something terribly wrong.

It was not until she peered out the front window did she realize that an auto had pulled up to the farm.

Her jaw dropped suddenly as she recognized Samuel jump from the driver's seat and hurry through the rain toward the door.

Joanna had already left for school and Rachel was alone in the house, working on her quilt.

What is he doing here? She wondered but there was no fear in his arrival. If anything, she felt a slight excitement.

"Did you forget something?" she asked, staring at him quizzically as stepped onto the front porch.

"Yes," he replied. "I forgot my manners."

She eyed him in confusion.

"Your manners?" she echoed. He shrugged sheepishly and Rachel realized that he was wet despite the short distance from the car to the door.

"Come in," she urged. "I will make coffee."

Am I making a mistake allowing him inside? She wondered but in her heart, she could not reconcile Samuel Baker with darkness.

He was a man in pain, that much was clear but why?

"Thanks," he told her, sitting at the kitchen table. "Listen, I thought about it and I know I probably scared you when I left yesterday."

Rachel glanced at him.

"It was abrupt, yes," she replied diplomatically. She did not tell him about her nightmare even though it had been plaguing her all day.

"I owe you an explanation," he said.

She placed two cups of coffee on the table, offering cream and sugar before sitting across from him, ready to listen.

He stared at her for a long moment and Rachel could sense that he was gathering his courage to put the words together.

Exhaling, he started.

"Once, a long time ago, I had a successful landscaping company in Detroit. I had clients in the suburbs and I did very well. I was married. My wife's name was Holly and we had a daughter."

Rachel felt her heart begin to race as she studied his face.

"One night, I came home from work, exhausted. Holly wanted to go out with friends and she left me alone with our daughter. I put her to bed and made myself something to eat."

Samuel stopped talking, his voice choked with emotion.

"I must have fallen asleep because when I opened my eyes, the house was on fire. Flames were licking my face but all I could think about was my baby girl. I raced toward the stairs, unaware of the burns and the blisters..."

Rachel's hand flew to her mouth and she gasped.

"There were no stairs left. There was no way to the second floor. The firefighters dragged me from the house, screaming in pain but not from the charred flesh. Holly stood in the night, staring at me and I will never forget the look on her face."

Samuel hung his head. Rachel could see him visibly shaking.

"She never forgave me. How could she? Brittany was dead because of me."

"It was an accident," Rachel murmured. "You did everything you could."

Samuel shook his head.

"No, I didn't. I couldn't take the aftermath. The guilt ate me alive. I filed for a divorce even though Holly needed me to mourn the loss of our daughter. I ran and I could never go back."

Rachel could not stop the tears from falling down her cheeks, trying to imagine the loss of her child.

"How can anyone be expected to handle such a situation well?" she asked quietly. Samuel laughed shortly.

"I heard she has remarried and had another child since. She has moved on. It seems I am the only one stuck in limbo."

Suddenly Rachel remembered Joanna's dream.

"Joanna dreamt about Brittany last night," she whispered. Samuel's head jerked up and his eyes narrowed slightly.

"Is that supposed to make me feel better?"

Rachel shook her head quickly, growing excited.

"No, she did. She told me the little girl in her dream was named Brittany and she saw you before the accident."

Samuel regarded her.

"Maybe Bishop Bachman was right," he mumbled, looking at his hands in embarrassment.

"What did he say?" she asked curiously.

"He thinks that God brought us together."

Their eyes met and a slow smile formed on Rachel's mouth.

"Please never repeat this to him," she whispered, taking Samuel's hand. "But Bishop Bachman is rarely wrong."

Samuel squeezed her palm gently.

"I look forward to learning that for myself," he replied.

As if his words were the anecdote, the humming in Rachel's ears subsided.

She could hear clearly again.

AN AMISH GIRL IN NEW YORK

It had taken months of begging and pleading to Mama and Papa, but they finally gave in. Ever since she was a little girl, Abby had an obsession with New York City. There was something about its bustling streets, towering buildings, and even its grit and grime that was so opposite to her small Amish community out in the countryside that unrelentingly called out to her. Each time her family passed through neighboring towns on their way to some market or trade show, she'd soak up every billboard and image depicting the towering skyline of the city that never sleeps.

Abby's parents always thought of her fascination with the city as a passing phase, something all young girls go through in some form or another, but once she turned sixteen she began talking more seriously about leaving home. Mama and Papa went away on rumspringa themselves when they were around her age, but they were still nervous thinking about their only daughter running off to the big city. At first, they insisted she pick a smaller, less intimidating city to visit, like Philadelphia or even Chicago where they had family that could keep on eye on her, but Abby was relentless. They tried to convince her to wait until her younger cousin was old enough to go with her to no avail. Abby had been waiting to go to New York City for as long as she could remember and once she turned eighteen she decided she couldn't wait a single second longer.

That morning, bags packed and dressed for travel, Abby sat down at the breakfast table and told her parents that she was leaving that day, with or without their permission. Not wanting to harbor any ill feelings toward their daughter or to explain to their neighbors that she ran off against their wishes, Mama and Papa gave in with a collective defeated sigh. Abby jumped up like a shot and hugged both her parents at once, almost knocking them to the floor.

"Thank you, thank you, thank you! I promise I'll be okay. Sarah's cousin has an apartment in Manhattan and she said I could stay with her for as long as I want and you don't even have to worry about money because Sarah says everyone in New York serving food at restaurants and it would be super easy for me to get a job, even without any experience or anything. I'll write to you every day, or every other day, or when I have time. It's New York, after all. I'm going to have so much to do! It's all so exciting!"

Abby flashed her parents a bright, enthusiastic smile that they tried to replicate, but their nerves stood in the way. Sarah was Abby's best friend from school. Her parents never let her go on rumspringa because of her cousin, Grace. Grace left home to visit the city when she was eighteen and never came back. Sarah's family was devastated, but Sarah kept in touch with Grace and was assured that she was happy and had made the right choice. Sarah's parents didn't want to take the risk that she might do the same.

"Just...be careful. Remember what you have waiting for you back at home."

"Listen to your Mama. This will always be your home. God has a path set for you here."

Abby brushed off her parents' words of caution with a closed-lipped smile and a small shrug. She understood their concern, but a week, or month, or year in New York wouldn't change her fundamental beliefs, and if it did would that automatically be a bad thing? Grace has lived in New York and away from the church for five years now and she was still a good person. Why did being Amish mean she had to hide herself away from the rest of the world her whole life? If she didn't go see the city she's dreamed of her entire life now then she never would. Besides, she was pretty sure she'd come back home. Her parents shouldn't worry so much.

Mama and Papa insisted she stay for one last meal before she caught the bus one town over that said "New York City" on the front. Abby could barely sit still long enough to bring bites of food to her mouth without shaking them off her fork. She'd seen that bus come and go hundreds of times, but that was the day she'd be going with it. Her mother tried to keep up a normal conversation, but Abby could only respond with "yes" or "no." Her mind was officially elsewhere. Eventually her father excused her from the table and she almost ran right out the door, but a small pang in her stomach stopped her at the threshold. Abby was unquestionably excited to start her journey, but she realized that she would miss her parents along the way. She slowed down for a moment to hug them both goodbye.

"Mama, Papa, I love you both very much. I'll see you when I get back."

She added that last part mostly to reassure her parents, but also a little bit for herself. She'd always imagines what might happen if she decided to stay in New York. She'd work hard to become an actress on Broadway, and one night a handsome fan would come to her dressing room after a particularly stirring performance and confess his love for her. It would turn out that he came from a rich family, of course, and even though she could absolutely support herself being a successful actress and all, she'd be in love and carefree for the rest of her life in a Manhattan penthouse. That was all a harmless fantasy, but the walk to the bus stop was absolutely real. An ounce of nervousness mixed with the excitement swirling around in her head.

She made it just on time, walked on to the half-filled bus, handed her ticket to a stone-faced bus driver and found a seat by the window. She wanted to see every inch of the city as they drove into it. An older woman with a lap full of knitting sat next to her and smiled. The familiarity calmed her a bit. Her mother spent the weekends knitting one and purling two after the morning's chores were finished. It would be a few hours before the skyline even came into view and the slow rocking of the bus soon lulled Abby to sleep.

Two or three hours later, she wasn't sure exactly, a particularly large bump in the road jostled Abby awake. The woman next to her was still knitting what now looked like a child-sized sweater. A quick look out the window revealed the view she'd been dreaming of for eighteen years. Abby clutched the small backpack she brought packed full of all her possessions to her chest and gasped. It was exactly like the pictures, but it also wasn't. Nothing could have prepared her for the jagged line of towering buildings that rose up out of the ground in front of her. The old woman chuckled.

"First time in New York City, dear?"

"Is it that obvious? I've always wanted to visit, but this is the first time my parents actually let me on a bus."

"Well, I prefer the quiet of the country now, but I spent a fair amount of my younger years wandering through the city streets. My daughter lives in Manhattan, so when I visit I get live vicariously through her. I can never stay for too long, though. These old bones can't withstand the hustle and bustle like they used to. Stay out all night for me at least once, will you? There's nothing like Times Square once all the tourists have gone back to their hotels."

Abby tried to assure her that she was going to do everything in New York, especially Times Square, but the woman seemed to lose herself in the memory, smiling down at the knitting in her lap. Abby didn't mind the sudden end to their conversation, it only assured her that sometimes just thinking about being in New York City was better than whatever you were actually doing. Her nails dug into the sides of her backpack as she tried to contain her excitement.

Sarah had given Grace all of Abby's bus information: bus number, time of departure and arrival, where it was going to drop her off. She promised to meet her there and help her figure out the subway.

"I can probably do it on my own. She don't have to go out of her way," Abby had said to Sarah, but Sarah said Grace had laughed kindly and told her there was no way she was going to let an Amish teenage girl get lost in New York on her very first day.

"She might end up wandering around Coney Island and I won't have that."

The streets started to narrow as the bus made it's way deeper into the city and closer to their destination. They passed small corner stores with yellow banners marked "Deli Grocery," and pop-up street vendors selling flowers or fruit or both. Abby tried to remember the face of every new person she saw. Everyone was so different here than in her homogeneous Amish community back home and she loved it. Each unique face had a different story behind it. What did the woman without shoes dressed all in tie-dye do all day? What about the old man in a crisp, tailored suit who read a book while he walked? She loved this city and she hadn't even stepped off the bus yet.

At the bus stop, she recognized Grace right away. Not only could she have been Sarah's somehow older twin, but she was also holding a big poster board sign that said, "Welcome to the Big Apple, Little Amish Girl!" Grace must have recognized her, too, because the moment Abby stepped off the bus she sprinted over and wrapped her in a huge hug, dropping the poster into the street.

"You're finally here! Welcome, welcome, welcome! I'm so excited to have someone from back home come visit me. I love it here, but there's something comfortable about that little town, huh? You excited? You ready for your stay at Casa de Grace?"

Abby knew Grace was kind and outgoing from Sarah's descriptions of her, but she had no idea how energetic she was. Going from the quiet, slow-talking lifestyle back home to Grace's immediate exuberance matched only by the city's chatter behind her was a little overwhelming for her. She could only manage an enthusiastic smile and nod while stumbling over the words, "Yes, okay, I'm ready!" Grace released her from the hug, picked up her sign with one hand, and locked hands with Abby with the other. Abby watched Grace's free-flowing curly hair bounce along behind her as she chatted about everything she wanted to do together while Abby was here. She had dyed it red and let it loose after moving to the city, and Abby admired it. Her dusty blonde locks were almost always pinned tightly to the back of her head and hidden under a bonnet. She left the bonnet at home this time, but the pins remained. She wondered if Grace would help her dye her own hair, maybe black, or blue even. Her parents would love that.

Grace excitedly rattled on about Strawberry Fields in Central Park, and eventually making it to the Statue of Liberty because she hasn't been there in ages, and of course they had to see a Broadway show, there were supposed to be a couple good ones premiering soon, never letting go of Abby's hand. A couple of blocks later, they descended into a subway station and stopped at an automated kiosk to purchase a MetroCard. Abby had never interacted with a machine this complex before and almost froze, not quite knowing what to do with the ball of crumpled bills in her hand. Luckily, Grace was quick to remember what life back home was like and thoughtfully helped her through the process. Holding the bright yellow and blue card in her hand made her feel very grown up and independent. She even made it through the turnstile on the first try.

"You're a natural, Abby! You were made for New York," exclaimed Abby.

Maybe I am, Abby thought.

Mama and Papa may have had more to worry about than a daughter with blue hair.

Grace took a break from listing every attraction in New York City to look down at her cell phone as they took their seats. Abby wrapped her arms tightly around the backpack on her lap and looked around the half-filled car. The subway was a completely new experience for her. She had never been on a bus before, either, but she had seen buses and the types of people on them. *This is like, an underground bus,* she told herself, not completely comfortable with being so far beneath the earth. She focused on the other people sharing the car. Just like the people on the street, no two of them were exactly the same. A tattooed mother sat quietly bouncing a child in her lap, while a teen a few seats down mirrored that image with a boom box blaring hip-hop.

Abby jumped as the train began to move. Grace chuckled and put a hand on her arm.

"I did the same thing on my first subway ride. Turned out I was on the right train but headed the wrong way so I had bigger fish to fry than dealing with being on a train for the first time," she threw back her head and laughed at the memory. "Once I realized I was no where near where I wanted to be I got off the train and started asking people which train would take me where I needed to be and they just kept telling me the one I was on. I didn't realize that the train going in the right direction was just on the other side of the platform. Man, did I feel dumb, but you won't have to worry about that, you have me!"

The two girls chatted for a little while as the train made it's way to their stop. Once they emerged back onto the city streets Abby began to get a feel for the constant flow of people. She quickened her pace to match Grace's and only bumped shoulders with a handful of people as she weaved through the crowd. Eventually, they walked into a tall building where a man sat at a desk by the door.

"Morning, Fred! This is my, well, she's basically my cousin. Abby's gonna be staying with me for a while so don't surprised if she comes flying through here at all hours of the day, okay?"

"Not a problem, Gracie! A friend of yours is a friend of mine. Nice to meet you, Abby!"

Abby smiled and waved at him as they walked to the elevator. She was surprised at how friendly everyone seemed to be. On the odd occasion that she did get her parents to talk with her about New York all they had to say about it was how unwholesome and rude the people were. She'd have to tell them how wrong they were when she got back. *If* she went back.

"That's my doorman, Fred. He's awesome. Always happy to see you even in the middle of the night. If you get yourself locked out or something and I'm not around Fred will help you out."

"That's good to know, thanks. Is everyone in New York this friendly?"

Grace laughed again.

"Not at all. Don't get me wrong, you'll find friendly people if you look for them but a lot of people would run you over with their cars and never look back. They're not bad people, they just have things to do and places to be and no time to stop and check if you're alive or not. That's your problem."

Grace saw a look of dismay cross over Abby's face.

"Don't worry, though. I'll make sure to introduce you to all the best people in New York. You just make sure not to get hit by any cars."

The elevator dinged as they made it to the fourteenth floor. Grace's apartment was at the end of the hall. It had two bedrooms, both with views overlooking the busy streets below, a small kitchen, a bathroom to share, and a living room filled with paintings and posters and a million other colorful decorations. Abby noticed a picture of Grace and Sarah from years ago sitting on a table by the couch. Before she could walk over to get a better look, Grace waved her into one of the two bedrooms. The room had a few pieces of art on the walls, but wasn't near as covered as the living room. A small bed was pushed up against the wall and dresser sat across from it with a TV placed on top.

"This is your room! I moved a bunch of stuff out of it and into the living room so you wouldn't be overwhelmed. I've only been here for a couple of years but I've managed to collect so much junk. I guess that's what happens when you go from a simple Amish life on the family farm to the big city. I can show you how to use the TV, too. I wouldn't blame you if you spent your first couple of days here just sitting in front of it watching cartoons. I know I did."

It was tempting, but Abby had been waiting to be a part of this city for so long she almost felt cooped up just being in the room to drop her things off.

"I'll definitely watch some TV later, but right now all I want is to explore or maybe find I job. I promised my parents I wouldn't ask them for money."

"Oh! I forgot to tell you. I know the manager of the diner down the street. He said he was looking for waitresses so I told him about you. He wants you to come down tomorrow morning so he can make sure you're not a total klutz or anything but you've basically got the job! How do you feel about pancakes?"

"I love pancakes! Thank you so much, Grace. You've done too much already."

"Don't even worry about it. I know what it's like being cooped up on a farm with no electricity or entertainment or fun. I want to make sure you're trip is the complete opposite of that! All fun, all the time. So, what do you want to do first?"

They spent the rest of the day just walking around Manhattan. They stopped for coffee at a sidewalk café, bought a few outfits fit for work at a department store, watched the dogs run around at the dog park. It was a fairly average day in New York but to Abby it was the best day of her life. Grace was a wealth of information, only stopping the flow to take sips of her latte. She knew the best place to get a burger, the best place for live music, the best cup of coffee – this wasn't it, but it would do.

"It's almost dinner time so why don't we start with the best Chinese takeout and spend the evening just hanging out at my place. How does that sound? You must be exhausted!"

She was exhausted, but she'd never admit it. She could only agree that Chinese food did sound good, even though she'd never had it before, and she wouldn't mind a night in. They stopped at a hole-in-the-wall restaurant only distinguishable by its vaguely oriental décor. Grace never once looked at the menu as she rattled off a list of food: crab rangoons, fried rice, sweet and sour chicken, lo mien, and don't forget the fortune cookies! When they got back to the apartment, Grace spread the feast out on her coffee table, handed Abby a pair of chopsticks, and said "Dig in!" After some fumbling with the sticks, she was able to shovel mountains of delicious and greasy food into your mouth.

While they watched the movie "Mean Girls," one of Grace's favorites, Abby broke open a fortune cookie. One side listed a handful of lucky numbers and the other said, "A big surprise is coming your way." She had spent so much time planning for this trip, accounting for every little detail, she wondered what surprises the city could possibly have in store for her. She could hardly sleep that night thinking about it. Maybe she wouldn't get the job. Maybe New York wouldn't live up to her expectations, but that couldn't be it because they already had. Maybe it would be something else, something so surprising that she couldn't even imagine it yet. She hoped that was it.

***

In the morning, Grace woke Abby up with a gentle shake and a steaming cup of coffee.

"Morning sunshine! It's your first day of work and I don't want you to be late. Here, I made you some coffee and I picked out an outfit for you last night, but you don't have to wear it. Sorry I'm acting like such a mom after you came all this way to get away from your parents. Yikes!"

Abby laughed, "I wasn't running *away* from my parents, I was running *to* New York! Thank you for the pleasant wakeup call."

"Well, I was definitely running from my parents. Living in that house was stifling; all those rules, no fun, and for what? God's plan? Sorry, I just get a little frustrated sometimes thinking about all the things my parents kept from me back home. I still feel religious from time to time, but the rigid rules of Amish life just aren't for me."

"Yeah, I know what you mean. I feel like there's so much I want to do that I just can't there. That's why I wanted to come here. I want to get it all out of my system so that I can go back to living simply. Once I've done everything I'll probably be so exhausted that I'll want to go back anyways!"

Grace smiled at her kindly, but bit her tongue. She knew better than most that it didn't always work that way. She didn't want to influence Abby's choice either way, but life as she saw it couldn't just be flushed out of someone's system. A person either craves an Amish life, or an English one. Abby just had to decide which it was she wanted most.

"We can talk about the serious stuff later. Why don't you jump in the shower and get ready for work while I cook breakfast. Go ahead and use whatever you find in there. Mi shampoo es tu shampoo!"

Abby washed herself, changed into the clothes Grace picked out for her, and played around with her makeup. Back home she didn't have any of this stuff. You didn't need makeup to go to church. Plus, every boy she knew had known her since they were children. They'd just be confused if she showed up to the Sunday sing one day covered in powders and creams, but here, no one knew her. She could wear as much or as little makeup as she wanted and no one would question it. Abby decided to start small, only applying a small amount of blush and a couple coats of mascara. The thick frame of lashes made her eyes look huge and the soft pink on her cheeks gave her the appearance of being a little bit warm. Even this small amount of makeup looked jarring in the mirror, but she also kind of liked it.

When she finally emerged from the bathroom Grace was dancing around her kitchen using a spatula as a microphone. At the end of an exaggerated spin she saw Abby standing in the hall giggling.

"Hey! You look awesome! You even threw on some makeup? That's advance level stuff. Now you just need to learn to flirt a little bit and you'll be swimming in tips."

"I know how to flirt!" Abby said defensively.

"Ha! Staring at a boy across the room during prayer is not flirting. New York's a completely different world."

"Oh yeah? How different can city boys be?"

"You know what? You might be right. All you have to do is blink those big doe eyes at one of these too-cool-for-school guys and they'll be smitten. You'll do fine."

"I don't even know if I want to date anyways."

"Oh, you'll change your mind the first time a cute boy tells you he likes your smile. Trust me. It happens to the best of us."

They talked a little bit about boys and back home over breakfast before it was time for Abby to head to the diner. It was so close to Grace's apartment building that she brought Abby down to the lobby, pointed to the place on the corner, sent her on her way and told her to ask for a man named Greg. She was a little nervous to go on her own, but this was exactly the experience that she was hoping to have in New York. Abby craved a taste of independence and she was finally getting it.

The diner was called "Rizzo's Place" and it looked exactly how she'd pictured a classic New York diner. The tables and chairs were all covered in turquoise vinyl complete with little flecks of glitter and the wait staff were all wearing crisp white aprons and matching paper hats. The aprons reminded her of her mother's back home, but that was the only ounce of familiarity she felt. The restaurant was fairly busy. Early morning was their rush hour, but that had passed so only a handful of stragglers and early lunch-eaters remained. She was standing by the doorway when a man only a little older than her wandered over to see if she wanted a table.

"Hey there! Can I help you?"

"I'm looking for Greg. I'm supposed to start working today."

The man's face broke out into a huge smile and he leaned in for a hug.

"You must be Abby! Grace told me all about you and how hardworking and great you are. Grace and I are like this," he crossed his fingers to show that they were close, "so I'd do anything for that girl. Oh! I'm Greg by the way."

Abby gathered from his tone that he might be gay. She had met one gay boy before back in her town, but he hadn't told anyone aside from her and a few friends about his sexuality. It wasn't something that bothered her, but seeing a man so openly flamboyant surprised and encouraged her. She had always thought of New York as a place where everyone could be exactly who they wanted to be, and seeing this man live up to that ideal was exciting. Abby smiled back and nodded.

"That's me! Thank you so much for giving me this job."

"You're so cute! Abby, you're going to fit in just fine here. I almost don't even think I have to train you. Want to just throw on an apron and dive right in?"

When a nervous look crossed over Abby's face he added, "All you have to do first is introduce yourself and ask if they'd like anything to drink. They usually just want coffee or water. If they want coffee make sure to ask about cream and sugar. I'll only give you one table for now so don't worry! If you flop, I'll be here to help you out but you seem like a natural!"

Greg scoped the restaurant to see which table he wanted to throw at her.

"Okay, there's one guy sitting in the corner. He's a regular. He usually just comes in for a coffee, sometimes scrambled eggs with a side of bacon, but nothing too complicated. Nice guy. Are you ready?"

Abby nodded. Greg smiled and gently pushed her forward. She didn't realize how quickly she'd be thrown into the actual serving part of the job, but she wasn't about to embarrass herself so she threw back her shoulders and approached the table as confidently as she could.

"Hey there! I'm Abby. Can I get you a coffee to drink? I mean, can I get you anything?"

From far away she couldn't tell how subtly attractive the man in the booth was. He was partially hidden by a beanie hat and an oversize sweatshirt, but when she got closer Abby could see a sharp jaw line and kind eyes beneath the baggy outerwear. She was thrown off by her attraction for a moment, but her desire to impress her new boss prevailed. She flashed him a professional smile as she bit her tongue.

"Yeah, sure, a black coffee would be great."

"Can I get you anything else?"

"Not right now, thanks."

She turned on her heal and walked back to Greg, not sure where she was supposed to take the order. Luckily, he was watching enthusiastically from the sidelines cheering her on silently.

"How'd it go? Was he nice? What am I saying, he's always nice! What did he order?'"

"Just a black coffee."

"Yep, that sounds like him. Let me show you where the coffee station is."

Greg helped her find the station and pour a cup. He showed her where the cream and sugar was, just in case her next customer needed it. He then showed her how to use the computer system in order to keep track of what each customer ordered. This was all very simple, however, and it wasn't long until she was right back at her only customer's table with the cup of coffee.

"Here you are, sir. One cup of black coffee."

"Thanks, but why are you talking like that. It sounds like you're a robot who was programmed to work in a diner."

Abby blushed.

"Oh, well it's my first day. Sorry. I'm still trying to get the hang of things."

The customer looked a little embarrassed as well. He didn't mean to call her out.

"No, I mean, I'm sorry. I didn't mean to embarrass you. Thanks for the coffee. It's great, as always."

Abby gave him a polite, but uncomfortable, half smile and turned to walk away but he stopped her.

"Wait, what's your name?"

"Abby."

"Abby, like Abigail?"

"No. Just Abby, actually. My mom just liked Abby."

"That's a nice name. Mine's Mac, like Mackenzie. My mom wanted a girl, but got me instead, so she picked a gender-neutral name. I don't mind it, though."

"I like Mac. There aren't a lot of guys where I'm from with names like that."

"Oh yeah? Where is it that you're from?"

"It's a little Amish town just outside of here, actually. I just got into the city yesterday."

"Yesterday? You need someone to show you around then."

Abby blushed again. She thought about what Grace said about flirting for tips, but this felt more genuine than that. This guy, Mac, didn't seem to care about tips.

"I'd like that."

"Great! Give me your phone number and I'll call you up sometime."

"Oh, I don't have a phone number. I don't have a phone."

"That's right. The whole 'Amish' thing. Well, when do you get off here?"

Greg had been listening in the whole time and jumped into the conversation.

"Right now! She's done for the day, wasn't she amazing? I just have to teach her how to clock out and she'll be on her way!"

Greg pulled Abby to the side to chat, but Abby was confused.

"Did I do something wrong? Do you not want me to work here?"

"No! No, of course not. I've just seen this guy come in day in, day out and, don't get me wrong he's one of the nicest customers we have which is why I'm doing this, but he's never once brought in a date or left with one. It's just so cute seeing you two together I can't resist! Go! Have a good time and come back tomorrow and we'll give you some real training. It was my mistake for giving you the cute, single guy as your first table."

Abby almost didn't know what to do. She expected to start her first job, but instead she was going on her first date. She walked back over to Mac's table, Greg casually waving his hands to encourage her.

"Sorry about that. It looks like I'm free now."

"Great! I can take you to work with me then."

Abby had no idea what this entailed but Greg gave her a thumbs up and she followed Mac out of the diner. They walked for a few blocks, casually chatting about their lives. Mac was very interested in Abby's Amish community and Abby was very interested in where Mac was taking her. If it hadn't been for Greg's insistence, she probably wouldn't have felt comfortable following a man she just met through New York City, but she couldn't resist. Eventually, he led them into a building and up a few flights of stairs. Greg pulled back a sliding iron door to reveal a colorful studio filled with paintings and sculptures.

"This is where I work, and live, I guess."

"You're an artist!" Abby exclaimed.

"I'd like to think so, but I've been in a rut lately. I haven't been able to create anything new. I don't want to sound cliché, but would you mind if I tried painting you? You haven't even taken off your work apron yet and your eyes are just so beautiful."

He didn't comment on her smile, but Grace's words still ran through her mind as this boy asked if she'd model for him. On one hand, she was weary, but on the other his sincerity penetrated through most else. She didn't feel as though he wanted anything from her except for her image so she agreed. Mac and Abby sat mostly still for the next couple of hours as Mac swept acrylics across a large canvas, capturing Abby in that moment. When the painting was finally done he turned it around and approached her.

"Alright, here it is. How do you like it?"

Abby looked at herself, carefully depicted in paint. Mac had noticed her mascara covered eyes, but hadn't painted them in a cartoonish way. He'd only enhanced the features on her face that had already been beautiful.

"It's...gorgeous! Is that conceded to say?"

"No, not when you look like you do."

Mac leaned towards Abby to kiss her. She almost turned away, but her instincts took over. With his mouth on hers she finally felt free of her parents grasp and also just free in general. He pulled away before she was finished enjoying the moment.

"I don't want to overstep my boundaries here. I like you a lot, but where from two different worlds."

Abby smiled confidently for the first time and touched his face.

"This is exactly what I want," she said before leaning back in to finish the kiss.

***

The two teens dated for a few weeks after that first studio session. Abby posed for multiple paintings, some more revealing than others, but always with her expressed consent. She loved having her freedom. She loved being able to come and go from Grace's apartment as she wished, but eventually she got bored. One night, as Mac painted Abby holding a bouquet of roses while sitting on a couch, she finally hit her breaking point. She threw the roses up into the air and started to shout.

"Mac! I can't do this anymore. What's the point of me coming here, day after day, just to be your model?"

"You're gorgeous, Abby. You're my muse!"

"But what am I getting out of this? Where does this take me?"

Mac couldn't answer that and Abby got up to leave.

"This has been fun, Mac, but I don't have a purpose here. I think I need to go home."

Mac tried to convince her to stay. He tried to convince her that her portraits meant more to him than just simple trinkets, but she wasn't swayed. As fun as the city was, as much freedom as she had, home would always be back in her little farm town. God had always had a path laid out for her, and this turned out to be only a detour.

SECOND CHANCE SWEETHEARTS

STEPHANIE SWIFT

Amanda changed her position in the leather chair for what felt like the hundredth time. *Legs crossed. Legs uncrossed. Fingers laced on top of her lap. Arms draped over the armrests.* Nothing felt comfortable, and it didn't help having sheriff Tucker's numerous commendations and trophies splayed across the shelves on the wall behind his desk. With just two years of police work under her belt, she couldn't help but wonder if she would ever see the day when her office in Atlanta, Georgia was littered with such accolades.

Amanda turned to her right and looked out the glass window separating sheriff Tucker's office from the rest of the precinct, where several deputies were busy answering phones and doing paperwork. Then again, her anxiety could be due to the fact she was in her hometown of Dayton, Ohio again – the last place on earth she wanted to visit. If it wasn't for the sheriff tracking her down and asking for her assistance on a case, she would've laughed at the invitation.

It's just business, Amanda. Get this done and you can be on the next flight back to Atlanta.

Amanda closed her eyes and took a deep breath just as sheriff Tucker swung open the office door. She's almost forgotten how big and surly the man was. His body literally filled the entire doorway, and he still had a scowl on his face – something that hadn't changed since her childhood. Had the man ever smiled? Somehow, she doubted it.

"Miss Miller, it's good to see you again," he remarked, as he made his way to the chair behind his desk and sat down. "I'm sorry to keep you waiting, but we've been running at full-speed with Paul Edison's murder investigation."

Amanda furrowed a brow. "Sheriff Tucker, you've known me since the day I was born. Please call me Amanda."

Still...no smile. Not even a smirk.

"I understand you couldn't share a lot of information over the phone, but I'm not sure why I'm here," she continued. "Paul and I went to school together, but I've never considered us close friends, so I really don't know how I can help you."

The sheriff leaned forward in his seat and rested his arms on top of his desk. He intertwined his fingers and remained quiet for several agonizing seconds, which didn't help her nerves at all.

"Miss Miller...*Amanda*...I'm not going to beat around the bush, because I don't believe in wasting time. The stab wound and other details associated with Mr. Edison's death are very similar to Micah's, and I feel like you would be an asset to this investigation. Your captain in Atlanta had nothing but praise for you."

As soon as the sheriff mentioned her brother, Amanda felt as if she'd been kicked in the gut. She shifted in her seat – again – and cleared her throat before attempting to speak.

"My brother's murder was never solved, so I'm still not sure how I can assist you with this case. Do you have some new leads?"

He looked down at his hands, as if contemplating his next words carefully.

"No, but having been raised with the Amish, I'm sure you remember how they don't care for our presence there, even when we're investigating the death of one of their own."

Amanda swallowed past the lump in her throat. She understood all too well what he meant. Memories of her father's confrontations with the officers following her brother's death drifted through her mind and made her cringe. If there was ever a defining moment that led to her leaving the faith and starting a new life with the English, that would be the one.

"Sheriff Tucker, I was shunned from the community when I left four years ago, so I seriously doubt they will welcome me back, even to help with this investigation. You and your deputies would probably have more luck getting information than I would."

He let out a deep sigh and nodded. "I'm aware of that, but we have to try. Their lives are in danger, and I'm not letting this killer get away with this – not again."

Amanda wanted to say no and be on her way to the airport, but the sheriff seemed so downtrodden and helpless, she hated to just walk away. Perhaps, by some miracle, she could get her old neighbors and friends to open up and talk to her, but she didn't want to put the cart in front of the horse. Right now, just finding a way into the community without the threat of backlash would be an accomplishment.

"Alright," she agreed, reluctantly. "I guess it's worth a shot, but I'm not making any promises."

That seemed to perk him up because he smiled – a real, honest to goodness smile. It was so odd seeing his lips curve into something other than a frown, Amanda didn't know whether to be thrilled or terrified.

"Good!" he exclaimed. "Let me get my keys, and I'll drive you to your mom and dad's house."

Amanda inhaled sharply and sat up a little straighter. Hopefully, she misunderstood him because there was no way she would step foot on her parents' property again – not after they practically disowned her when she decided to move.

"Why are we going there?" she asked.

He leaned back in his seat and gave her a quizzical look. "Your mother made it clear that you would stay with them if you came to town. They were the ones who helped me locate you."

Amanda closed her eyes and groaned. His answer didn't surprise her at all and sounded just like something her mother would say. She could argue with her parents and refuse to stay under their roof, but to what end? Fighting would only make things worse, and the situation was bad enough without throwing their family drama into the mix.

"Fine," she agreed. "Hopefully we'll be able to solve this case sooner rather than later."

If he wondered about her reluctance, he didn't mention it, and as they made their way out of the precinct to his squad car, Amanda tried to settle the jittery butterflies in her stomach by taking a couple of deep breaths.

It didn't help.

After four years of non-communication, she was going to be trapped in her parents' house for only God knew how long. Just when she thought her predicament couldn't get any worse…it did.

* * * *

Jacob saw the brown squad car coming down the dirt road long before the sheriff turned into the Miller's driveway and parked beside their house. As he pulled up on the reins and brought the plow horse to a halt, he caught sight of their daughter, Amanda, getting out of the passenger seat.

Jacob let out a low whistle. "This can't be good."

He'd worked for the Miller's only two short years, but he and Amanda went way back as childhood sweethearts. Although it excited him to see her again, he still got a bad feeling in the pit of his stomach. Shunned people didn't usually return to their Amish roots except under dire circumstances, and given the fact she arrived with the sheriff didn't bode well at all.

Jacob picked up the reins and motioned the horse toward the barn. He still had three more rows to complete before his work day was finished, but for reasons he couldn't explain, he felt a strong urge to find out what was going on. Since his wife's passing one year prior, William and Ruth Miller had practically become family, and perhaps it was none of his business, but he couldn't just stand by and do nothing. After all, it wasn't every day the sheriff decided to pay a visit.

Amanda was dressed in English clothing, and her long, wavy brown hair billowed in the wind as she walked to the front door. The pants and blouse she wore hugged her curves and Jacob shook his head and cleared his throat, which suddenly felt dry.

Stop it, Jacob. Don't even go there. The last thing he wanted or needed was to get involved with someone – especially someone who was chauffeured around by law enforcement and banned from their community, like Amanda.

Jacob tied the horse to a fencepost outside the barn and headed for the house. He removed a handkerchief from his trouser pocket and wiped the dirt and sweat from his brow. As he entered quietly through the back door, their voices carried down the long hallway from the living room, and he could tell immediately that Mr. Miller wasn't amused.

Jacob tip-toed to the restroom and washed his hands and face before making his way to the front of the house. Sheriff Tucker stood near the doorway with his arms crossed over his chest, while Amanda sat in a chair across from her parents, who were sitting on the sofa. The tension in the air was so thick you could cut it with a knife, and as every head turned his way when he walked in the room, he didn't know whether to stay put or retreat.

"I'm sorry, but this is a private conversation..."

William held up a hand to stop the sheriff from saying anything else, and even though it looked like it pained him, the officer quit talking.

"Jacob is like family. He can hear whatever you two have to say," he replied. "Jacob, I'm sure you remember Amanda."

The fact that he didn't address her as his daughter wasn't lost on him...or Amanda. He noticed the way she looked down at her feet and closed her eyes, and a part of him felt sorry for her. When she turned her attention back to her father, he could see the glisten of unshed tears in the corner of her eyes before she acknowledged Jacob with a nod.

"I know you don't want me here, and I don't blame you, but sheriff Tucker wouldn't have called me unless it was important. He...he believes that Paul Edison's death may in some way be connected to Micah's."

William never flinched, but Ruth reacted to the mention of her late son's name with a bowed head and muffled cries that made his heart ache. Amanda reached over and held her hand, and Jacob was relieved when Ruth squeezed it tight instead of pulling away.

"I appreciate you inviting me to stay here while we investigate, and I promise I'll try not to overstay my welcome."

William cast an angry glance at his wife, leaving Jacob to wonder if he'd been privy to the invitation, and when his gaze turned to Amanda, he assumed by his red face and rapid breaths that the answer was a solid "no".

"I don't know what you expect to find here, but your mother and I won't be pulled into any nonsense. Instead of questioning the good, God-fearing people here, you should turn your attention to Dayton. The English have no respect for others, and the murderer is probably among them."

Sheriff Tucker moved from his stance by the doorway, and there was no mistaking the contempt in his eyes.

"Mr. Miller, with all due respect, Paul Edison and your son were found in the woods surrounding this community. Now, I can't speak for every person in Dayton, but I can tell you I've never had a single report of an English man or woman endangering this neighborhood in the thirty years I've been sheriff here."

William grabbed his hat from the table beside the sofa and abruptly stood.

"Until now," he seethed. "I believe you know your way out."

Without another word, William stormed from the room and out the back door. When the screen door slammed shut, Jacob felt a cold chill race up his spine. In one sense, he felt like he should go after him, but he also couldn't seem to make his feet move.

"I'll get your suitcase from the car," Sheriff Tucker said.

He walked out the front door and the room became deathly still, except for the sound of Ruth's soft sobs. Jacob and Amanda exchanged glances, and he tried to lighten the mood by smiling at her, but the smile she gave him in return was weak and laced with sorrow. She didn't shed a tear, but the sadness in her demeanor was unmistakable.

"I'm so sorry, mom."

Ruth looked up at her daughter and gently touched her cheek. The sweet gesture brought a lump to Jacob's throat.

"Your father doesn't mean any harm, dear. He's just hurting."

Amanda nodded, and when the sheriff returned with her belongings, he attempted to turn the conversation to something more pleasurable. Ruth's tears stopped flowing, and Jacob thought he detected a smile when the sheriff mentioned sampling one of her pies at the farmer's market in Dayton, where she sold them to make some extra money.

Despite the happier atmosphere, Amanda remained quiet in her seat. He wanted to go to her, but he didn't know what he could possibly say that would make her circumstances less daunting. Perhaps it was best to just stay as far from the drama as possible.

Jacob groaned.

No, he became involved as soon as he made the unwise decision to walk in the room and stick his nose where it didn't belong. He hated to admit it, but there was no turning back now.

* * * *

"Rise and shine! It's almost time for church!"

Amanda sat up straight in her bed at the sound of her father's bellowing. She tried to adjust her eyes to the sunlight streaming through the window on the opposite side of the room, and she could barely make out her father's figure in the open doorway.

"Church?" she questioned. "You're joking, right?"

He walked in the room and threw open her closet door in one swift movement that made her head spin. "I never joke about church. Don't you have anything in here that looks decent?"

Amanda stood and walked over to the closet. "I appreciate the offer, but I don't think the neighbors would take kindly to an English woman joining their service."

When she closed the closet door, her father put his hands on his hips and gave her a stern look. She straightened her spine and jut out her chin, but instead of feeling like a grown woman, she felt like an unruly child being scolded for rolling around in the mud or getting their hand caught in a cookie jar.

"So, I take it you've completely abandoned your faith," he retorted. "Is that it?"

Amanda groaned as she went back to the bed and sat down. "No, I haven't. If you must know, I've been attending a wonderful Baptist church every Sunday since I moved to Atlanta."

He grunted as if her presence in some other church besides an Amish one was unspeakable and vile, and his self-righteous attitude angered her even more.

"Get dressed. We're leaving in ten minutes."

When he left the room, and slammed the door on his way out, Amanda bit her tongue to keep from screaming after him. It was her third day there, and she still hadn't received a kind word from him. Her mother, on the other hand, had welcomed her home with open arms.

As she took off her pajamas and slipped on the most "decent" dress she brought with her from Atlanta, Amanda let her mind drift to the interviews she'd conducted with the neighbors since her arrival. She had only a small handful of people left to talk to, and so far, she hadn't collected any clues. Paul Edison's widow was too distraught to offer much help, and bringing in a K-9 unit from Dayton to canvas the crime scene left them empty-handed too.

Amanda went to the restroom and brushed her teeth and hair as images of Jacob Troyer flashed through her mind. Besides sheriff Tucker, he was the only person who'd shown a genuine interest in helping, but that could've been more out of respect for her parents than anything.

"Amanda! We're leaving!" her father yelled.

Frustrated, Amanda hurriedly put on her shoes and joined them outside. There wasn't time to put on makeup, but that was probably a good thing, since the dress and high heels were more than enough for the neighbors to condemn her for.

Her mother smiled at her as she climbed into the wagon and sat down on the wooden seat beside her, but the ride to the church dragged on as her father brought any chance for pleasant conversation to a halt with his abrupt replies and grim attitude.

As soon as they approached the church, she could feel everyone's eyes upon her, but she squared her shoulders and shrugged it off. She received a few greetings from the parishioners standing outside, but their judgmental tones were unmistakable. Jacob met them as soon as they walked through the door, and she followed him to one of the empty wooden pews near the front of the sanctuary.

Amanda sat down between Jacob and her mother, and she felt a little more at ease. They were the only two people in the small community who didn't seem repulsed by her presence, so she soaked in their smiles, hoping it would lighten her mood. A few minutes before the service started, Amanda gazed around the room one last time and wasn't surprised to find the others whispering amongst themselves while casting glances her way. One woman, however, acted very peculiar.

"Jacob, who is that woman sitting on the back pew by the window?" she asked.

She stared straight ahead while Jacob casually turned in his seat and glanced toward the back of the church. "That's Faith Cullen. Her husband, Ben, is sitting beside her."

She hadn't interviewed them yet, and she couldn't recall how far down their names were on her list. While the others chatted away, Faith sat with her back rigid and her eyes focused on the Bishop's podium near the front of the church. The one time she did glance Amanda's way, Ben gave her a harsh look that made her cheeks redden, and she hadn't taken her eyes off the podium since.

"Why do you ask?" Jacob inquired. "Is something wrong?"

Amanda glanced at him, and she was immediately aware of how close they were. The church was packed to overflowing, leaving them squished together like sardines in a metal can, so there was no way to avoid touching him, but he didn't seem to mind. When he looked at her, she caught herself staring at his haunting blue eyes, his long eyelashes, and the faintest hint of dimples in his cheeks. Amanda fanned herself with a hymnal and tried to focus on something else besides the heat emanating from his body.

"Nothing's wrong," she replied. "I was just curious."

Thankfully, the Bishop entered the room at that time, so she had something else to focus her attention on, but the next two hours spent listening to his sermon passed by incredibly slow. She'd forgotten how tiring it was to sit on a wooden pew for an extended amount of time, and she missed the cushioned seats in her church in Atlanta. When the Bishop started his closing prayer, Amanda murmured a silent "thank you" to the heavens, knowing it would soon be over.

Her parents wasted no time in making their way to the exit as soon as the Bishop said "amen", but Amanda wanted to speak to the Cullen's before leaving. Jacob followed closely on her heels, and as they drew closer, she didn't miss the frightened look on Faith's face. Ben stood a few feet away, and if the woman hadn't been surrounded by such a large crowd, she probably would have bolted.

"Faith Cullen?" she asked. "Hello. I'm Amanda Miller."

She held out a hand to greet her, but Faith kept her arms crossed in front of her, fiercely clutching her Bible to her chest. Her lips moved, but no audible words came out, and as Amanda and Jacob shared confused glances, Ben suddenly appeared and pulled Faith close to his side.

"We know who you are," he stated.

His eyes were dark, and his attitude immediately ruffled her feathers. She'd seen enough bullies since moving to Atlanta it was easy now to spot one in her own hometown. He was a few inches shorter than most of the men in the congregation, but despite his shortcomings, he had an air about him that tried to demand respect. Amanda could tell right away he wouldn't be interviewed willingly.

"If you'll excuse us," he said. "Let's go, Faith."

He never released the death grip on her waist, and she looked like she'd seen a ghost. When they walked past her, Amanda could faintly hear her whispering, "Romans eight one...Romans eight one..."

As she and Jacob watched the two of them walk briskly toward the exit, she couldn't help but wonder what her babbling meant. *Romans 8:1 or was it chapter eighty-one of Romans? Was she referring to scripture or something else?*

"Well, that was strange," Jacob commented.

Amanda nodded, but she was too sidetracked by her own thoughts and questions to reply. Unfortunately, she didn't have a pen or pencil to write with, so she burned the phrase to her memory, determined to look it up as soon as she returned home.

Perhaps it was just senseless jabbering, but for reasons she couldn't explain, Amanda felt a tiny spark of hope – something she hadn't experienced since stepping foot in Dayton. With any luck, it would be a step in the right direction.

* * * *

The sun was getting ready to make its descent in the west when Jacob finally finished his work for the day. As he closed the barn doors behind him, every muscle in his body ached, but when he turned and spied Amanda sitting on the back-porch swing, he felt instantly rejuvenated. William and Ruth were visiting with friends and would be gone for at least a couple more hours, and the thought of being alone with Amanda was tempting. She looked lost in thought, and he contemplated leaving without interrupting her, but he was drawn to her like a moth to a flame, which both irritated and excited him at the same time.

After his wife's passing, he swore he'd never look at another woman the same way, but he'd noticed his resolve waning little by little since Amanda's arrival. He knew it was unlikely the two of them stood a chance at a rekindled romance, since they led very different lives, but there was no denying the way his body reacted whenever she was near. As he made his way to the back porch, his heartrate escalated and his palms became sweaty.

"Mind if I join you?" he asked.

Amanda jumped at the sound of his voice, and he immediately wished he'd listened to his conscious and headed home instead of bothering her. Her mind was definitely elsewhere.

"Sure," she replied, patting the empty space on the swing beside her.

He sat down on the opposite end, leaving enough space between them so she wouldn't get the wrong idea, even though he really wanted to sit right beside her. She was dressed in jeans, a t-shirt, and sneakers, and a long ponytail peeked from beneath the baseball cap she wore. Her face was clear of makeup, and her natural beauty took his breath away.

They sat in silence for a few minutes, but when she shifted her position on the swing, his heart fell to his feet when her shirt lifted slightly and he saw a pistol strapped to her side.

"Amanda, why do you have a gun?"

She glanced at it before pulling her shirt back down. "I wish I could tell you."

The ominous tone in her voice put him on edge and made his heart race for an entirely different reason. Normally, he would have dropped the conversation, since it was obvious she didn't want to talk about it, but something urged him onward. He understood the secrecy of her job, but that didn't stop him from worrying over her safety.

"Amanda, please talk to me," he pleaded. "I promise I won't breathe a word to anyone."

When she looked at him, he could see the inner battle raging in her beautiful hazel eyes, and when she didn't respond right away, he feared he may have overstepped his boundaries. She leaned forward and nervously rubbed her hands back and forth over her thighs before taking a deep breath.

"Did you hear what Faith said yesterday before she and Ben left the church?" she asked.

Jacob thought for a moment before shaking his head.

"She was whispering 'Romans eight one' repeatedly, so I looked it up when I got home. There's only sixteen chapters in the books of Romans, so she couldn't have meant 'chapter 81', and when I checked Romans 8:1, it read, *'There is therefore now no condemnation to them which are in Christ Jesus, who walk not after the flesh, but after the Spirit'.*"

She seemed deeply troubled by it, but he couldn't imagine why, so he didn't question it.

"I went to their house this morning to interview them about Paul Edison, and their wagon was in the driveway, but they wouldn't come to the door. I know they were home because I could hear their footsteps. I can't put my finger on it, but something's not right, and I'm going back to their house as soon as it gets dark."

Jacob cocked an eyebrow. "Why not right now? I'll go with you."

Amanda leaned back in the swing and pushed her feet against the wooden planks to set it in motion. The gentle sway of it made some loose tendrils caress her face and he fought the urge to tuck them behind her ear like he used to when they were younger.

"I'm afraid you don't understand, Jacob. I'm going to spy on them...not visit with them."

Her comment made the tiny hairs on the back of his neck stand at attention. The thought of her sneaking around the Cullen's house in the dark with a gun made his skin crawl. He didn't know them very well, but it was safe to say Ben probably owned a rifle like every other man in the vicinity.

"I'm still going with you," he repeated.

Amanda pressed her feet against the porch and stopped the swing, nearly jerking him out of it. Her eyes were wide and expressive, and she immediately started shaking her head.

"No, you're not. It's too dangerous, and if something happened to you I'd never forgive myself."

Jacob was caught between feeling offended over her refusal and happy over her concern for his safety. Regardless, he wasn't about to back down.

"Amanda, I know you do this for a living, and I get that, but I would never forgive *myself* if something happened to *you*, so we can do this the easy way or the hard way."

He could tell by the way she groaned and rolled her eyes heavenward that she was annoyed, but he didn't let that deter him. If she decided to never speak to him again after everything was said and done, he would have to find some way to live with that, but he couldn't just sit idly by and do nothing.

"Fine, but you'll follow my lead and do exactly as I say. Understood?"

He was so relieved he didn't care what kind of orders she barked at him, but as the sun went down and the darkness closed in around them, the gravity of their situation settled in his gut like a lead balloon.

Amanda refused to let him bring one of her father's rifles with them, and as they hopped off the back porch and began making their way to the main road, he felt vulnerable and ill-prepared. However, he'd never seen Amanda look so confident and in her element before.

The Cullen's homestead was a little over a mile away, but thankfully the moon guided their path and the road was clear of travelers. Neither of them spoke during their trek, and when the Cullen's house came into view, Amanda left the main road and cut a path through the field between the Cullen's and their next-door neighbor.

As they made their way slowly toward the house, Jacob's heart thumped wildly inside his chest when he heard the squeak of door hinges. Amanda grabbed his arm and pulled him to the ground, just as a light shone from the back door of the Cullen's home. Through the dense growth of weeds, they watched as Ben Cullen headed for the woods beyond the large field directly behind his house. He carried a lantern in his right hand, and Jacob swallowed hard when he saw the rifle in his left hand. When he was far enough away to follow without being spotted, Amanda gestured for Jacob to start moving again.

It seemed to take forever to reach the wooded area, but it couldn't have been more than just a few minutes. Amanda was agile and light on her feet, and if it wasn't for the moonbeams leading the way, he probably would have lost sight of her a dozen times. Ben's lantern shined brightly in the darkness several feet ahead of them, and as they continued to follow him, Jacob noticed they were on a clear path leading through the woods. Apparently, it was traveled quite often.

Ben stopped walking and Jacob nearly tripped over Amanda when she came to a sudden stop before pulling him behind a tall pine tree. He heard a faint clicking sound as she snapped open her holster, and when she removed the Glock, and then a small flashlight from her pants pocket, he was almost afraid to breathe. They both leaned to their right and peeked around the tree, and he was shocked when he saw Ben kneeling on the ground, digging a hole with his bare hands. A few seconds later, he pulled something from beneath his vest, and when the glow from the lantern glimmered off the blade of a large knife, he sucked in a breath.

"Stay here," Amanda whispered. "Don't move."

He nodded, and as she tip-toed her way toward Ben, he quickly scanned his surroundings for something he could use as a weapon, just in case he needed one. The only thing within reach was a fallen tree limb and a couple of small rocks, but before he had time to contemplate his next move, the bright light from Amanda's flashlight illuminated the area around him, and he heard her yell, "Ben Cullen! Drop the knife and put your hands in the air!"

The seconds that followed were a blur, but when Jacob heard the sound of gunfire, he called Amanda's name...and feared the worst.

* * * *

Amanda walked out of the interrogation room and was shocked to find her parents and Jacob sitting outside on one of the precinct benches, waiting for her. She was even more shocked when her parents rushed over and wrapped her in their arms.

"We've been so worried!" her mother exclaimed.

Amanda led the three of them down a corridor to an empty breakroom and closed the door behind them, so they wouldn't be disturbed.

"I'm sorry. I know I should've contacted you right away, but it's been chaotic around here between getting Ben to the hospital to bandage up his shoulder and then here for questioning."

Amanda felt like a heel when she saw how genuinely upset they were. Jacob stood quietly by and didn't utter a word, but she could see the wheels turning in his head even though he didn't speak.

"What did you find out?" her father asked.

Amanda motioned toward a table and chairs in the center of the room, and as they all pulled up a seat around it, she took a deep breath before trying to explain what had happened during the past eight hours since she arrested Ben.

"Faith is the one who told us Ben killed Paul...and Micah too. When Ben found out, he confessed to the murders."

Her mother covered her mouth with her hand and tried to stifle a cry while her father put his arm around her and held her close. Amanda cleared her throat to keep from crying.

"Faith said Ben was jealous of any man who paid too much attention to her, and he mistook Micah and Paul's friendliness for flirting and became enraged."

Her father pressed his lips so firmly together they turned white, and she could see the anger burning in his eyes. "We lost our son...our only son...over one man's *jealousy*? Over nothing?"

Amanda knew it was hard for them to fathom because she had a tough time understanding it too. She reached across the table and held their hands, wishing she could erase their pain. "I'm so sorry."

When her father squeezed her hand and smiled through his tears, she tried not to get her hopes up over it. "You solved your brother's case, and we're so proud of you, Amanda. Maybe now that his killer will be brought to justice we can start moving forward again."

Her mother nodded in agreement, and Amanda wanted to say something, but she was so overcome with emotion she was afraid talking would burst the dam and start an endless stream of tears. Instead, she stood and walked around the table so she could hug them both, and afterwards, while they comforted each other, she gestured for Jacob to follow her to the opposite side of the room, where he leaned against the window and looked out onto the street.

"I guess now we know why Faith kept repeating that scripture," he said.

Amanda frowned as she thought back to their conversation in the interrogation room. "He brainwashed her into thinking it was all her fault because 'her flesh was weak', but she never flirted with them – or any man for that matter. He's just an evil human being."

Jacob surprised her when he grabbed her hand, and Amanda felt her cheeks flush with excitement.

"It scared me to death when I heard the gunshot, and I thought you'd been hit," he replied. "I don't know what I would've done if something happened to you."

Amanda smiled at his remark. When Ben grabbed his rifle, and turned to fire it at her, she wanted to do more than just knock it from his hands by grazing his shoulder with a bullet, but somehow, she managed to contain her anger. The justice system would make him pay for his crimes, and she couldn't wait to see him locked behind bars for the rest of his life.

"So...I guess dating a cop is out of the question?" she asked.

She didn't miss the way his eyes lit up, and her heart leapt to her throat when he brought her hand to his mouth and gently kissed her fingers. "I never said that."

Amanda laughed softly as she gazed across the room at her parents. "I was hesitant about coming back here when sheriff Tucker called me, but I'm so thankful I did. I hope this means I finally have a family again."

Jacob tightened his hold on her hand. "I think this will be a new beginning for a lot of people – not just your parents. When my wife passed away, I didn't think I would ever be able to look at another woman the same way again, but that changed when I saw you again. I know we lead different lives now, but...I'm willing to give this another chance if you are."

Amanda tried to quell the butterflies in her stomach, but it was nearly impossible with him standing so near.

"I'm ready," she whispered.

As he gazed upon her with desire radiating from his mesmerizing blue eyes, she sighed contentedly while the heat from his touch coursed through her veins and made her weak in the knees. She had to admit...there was no place like home.

RACHEL

The air on her face was biting at her cheeks but she barely noticed it. A feeling of contentment had washed over her and the beauty of the picturesque landscape filled her with a joy she had never known.

Someone was calling her name and she whirled around, her skirt swirling around her ankles, a small smile on her face.

"Rachel!" he called again and she turned in the opposite direction, scanning the field at her back. Her dark hair was longer than it had ever been, cast in two long braids along either shoulder, a dramatic contrast to the white of her apron.

Despite the snow on the ground, her feet were bare and suddenly, she was painfully aware of how cold she had grown.

Gone was the sense of comfort in which she had been enveloped as something sinister filled the air instead.

"Rachel!" his voice was further away than it had been and again she spun but she no longer felt a sense of peace but an unsettling panic.

"Rachel!" the cry was desperate now, demanding and she twirled, a full circle, trying to identify the source.

Someone shoved her from behind and she gasped.

"Rachel!" The voice was directly in her ear now.

Her cobalt blue eyes flew open and she stared up at the furious face of the resident hovering above her.

"Are you kidding me?" Dr. Levin snapped. "You're taking a nap? Get up!"

Her heart racing, Rachel swung her legs over the side of the cot in the on-call room and rubbed her eyes, trying to shake off the dream.

"What happened?" she asked, jumping to her feet. She peered at her pager, her brow furrowing. It was unlike her to sleep through the vibration of the device but as she glanced at the screen, she saw that no one had paged her.

What is he doing in here? No one is looking for me.

"Car accident on Highway 80. Three badly injured. One dead."

Rachel hurried to follow the surly doctor from the room, trying to focus.

"Why wasn't I paged?" she asked and he cast her an annoyed look.

"I am telling you, aren't I? Why do you need to be paged?" he growled. "Why do you need to make everything difficult and ask stupid questions?"

Rachel had been a nurse at Saint Francis Memorial in San Francisco for two years. In that time, she had grown friendly with most of the ER staff. It was not hard to do with her sunny personality and warm smile but Dr. Levin was an anomaly.

He seemed to hate Rachel from the first minute he had laid eyes on her, going out of his way to make her life miserable.

His attitude was commonplace and both doctors and nurses rued having to work their shifts with him.

"Can you walk a little faster, please? People's lives are at stake while you take in the scenery," the resident yelled back, from five paces ahead.

Rachel bit the insides of her cheeks and rushed after him, pushing their way into the bustling emergency room.

It was her third double shift that week and she was exhausted. The nap she had been taking was the first sleep she had in over twenty hours and it had only lasted twenty minutes and been plagued by the strange dream.

As they arrived at the ambulance bay, she realized that the busses hadn't arrived yet.

"They aren't here yet?" she asked aloud.

"Oh, sorry," Dr. Levin snapped sarcastically. "Did you want to go back and take a nap until they get here?"

The other staff waiting gave him a reproving look, his sour attitude notorious among the others but Dr. Levin seemed impervious to their silent scolding.

Nancy, the head night nurse gave Rachel a warm smile as if to say, "don't worry about it" but Rachel had long since learned to deal with Dr. Levin's nastiness.

She smiled back at Nancy with false bravado.

It was nobody's business that Dr. Levin made her feel small and inept.

In minutes, the ambulances roared into port and the physicians were ready.

Rachel kept her ears perked for instructions, stepping out of the way to allow the doctors to do their jobs.

"Are you just going to stand there? Get this boy 5 milligrams of morphine stat!" Dr. Levin barked at her and humiliation colored Rachel's face. He was the only doctor who questioned her work ethic.

Swallowing her anger, Rachel turned to oblige his request, returning a moment later with a vial. She hurried toward the broken patient who was writhing in pain, moaning as tears slid down his cheeks. His shin bone was protruding from his leg and there was a deep gash on his chest.

"Oh, it hurts so bad," he cried. "Please, please help me!"

"Shh," Rachel murmured, preparing his vein. "You're going to feel better in a minute but you have to be still."

She steadied his arm to inject the needle when something caught her eye.

Quickly, she put the needle on the instrument tray and picked up his wrist.

"Please!" he moaned. "Make it stop!"

"Nurse King, are you going to administer that today?" Dr. Levin yelled, his face turning red with anger.

"I just – "Rachel protested, holding up the boy's slender wrist.

"Just give me that and get out of here."

Before Rachel could finish her statement, the boy fainted from the pain.

"Great! Nice work, Rachel. You're the most incompetent nurse I have ever seen," Dr. Levin raged, plunging the needle into the patient's arm.

"No!" Rachel gasped. "No! You're going to kill him!"

Dr. Levin turned away from her, ignoring her words and back to dealing with the bleeding gash on his chest.

"Dr. Levin!" she screamed.

"Nurse King, get out of here," he growled but Rachel didn't budge.

"No! He's going to go into anaphylactic shock! He's allergic to opiates."

She pointed at the medical alert bracelet on the patient's arm.

Dr. Levin went pale, shaking his head in disbelief and Rachel felt herself grow lightheaded.

Suddenly, his head whipped up and his eyes narrowed into slits.

"What did you do?" he hissed. Shocked, Rachel couldn't answer.

"You're incompetent! You'll never work in another hospital again!"

"Me?" she echoed, choking. "You're the one who – "

"Get out of here before you do more damage!" he roared, attracting the attention of all the other staff. "This is unforgiveable!"

Rachel backed away uncomprehendingly.

But I didn't do anything! I tried to stop him!

It was at that moment she realized that she was about to be blamed for what had happened.

"This is crap, Rachel! You need to fight this!"

Rachel stifled a sigh. It was the same conversation they had at least twenty times in the past three weeks.

"There's nothing left to fight, Cara. I've been stripped of my nursing licence. I can't practice in the state of California anymore."

"No! Dr. Levin is the devil! You can't let him get away with this!" her roommate insisted. "How can he do this?"

The question was also not foreign to Rachel; it had plagued her day and night since being called up on her review.

"They didn't believe me, pure and simple. Whose word were the going to take? A new nurse or a resident who had been at Memorial for seven years?"

"He's been written up like a million times!" Cara protested. "How can they disregard his history – oh Rach, I am so sorry I keep bringing this up but it is so unfair!"

Rachel finally turned to face her, smiling kindly.

"It's okay, Cara," she promised. "Maybe this is the universe's way of telling me I wasn't cut out for nursing after all. Two years in and I already feel like I'm burning out."

Yet as she said the words, there was a deep knife stabbing into her heart.

Rachel thought of how many hours she had worked studying, working two jobs to put herself through college.

And after college, working eighty or sometimes ninety-hour weeks.

The quest to get where she wanted to be had been excruciating and Dr. Levin had snatched it away with one swipe to save his own skin.

It was over before it had even really begun.

The only saving grace was that the young man had not suffered any long-term damage because of Dr. Levin's mistake.

If I hadn't brought it to his attention, he would have killed the boy.

Rachel knew it was only a matter of time before the doctor did kill someone.

"You can't go back to New York," Cara said dejectedly as Rachel continued to pack her bags. Rachel smiled tightly.

"I can't really afford to stay here without a job," she reminded her friend.

"You'll get another job, Rach. Just hang in there and start looking. You made up your mind without thinking it through entirely. I can cover the rent for – "

"No." There was a finality in Rachel's tone.

What had happened at the hospital had left her badly scarred and she knew she needed to distance herself from San Francisco for a while.

"No, Cara. Thank you for the offer but I think it's best that I go home to my mom and dad for a while. Clear my mind, you know?"

Cara nodded slowly but Rachel could see she did not understand.

Rachel didn't blame her for her confusion; she wasn't sure she comprehended her own willingness to leave either.

I'm burnt out. I need to regroup, collect my thoughts and figure things out. Maybe I'll end up back here but for now, I have to go.

"Walk me to the car?" she asked Cara with feigned cheer and her roommate sighed, nodding.

"Do I have a choice?" she replied sadly.

"Not if you want a really good hug."

Rachel picked up her oversized duffle bag and Cara reached for the last two boxes in the otherwise empty room.

The made their way to the U-Haul and loaded it.

"Will you call me when you get where you're supposed to be?" Cara asked, pulling Rachel into a tight embrace.

Rachel swallowed and nodded but she could not answer.

She wondered if she would ever find the place she was supposed to be.

She stretched out her long legs against the floral print of the comforter.

"No, mom, I'm fine, I swear," she said into the receiver. "I'll be home around noon tomorrow."

Rachel listened as her mother rattled off a list of precautions and rolled her eyes, a mixture of affection and annoyance tickling her stomach.

"Yes, I will make sure to eat...no, don't worry about the snow. I checked the weather before I left California...yes, the truck is reliable...okay mom, I love you too. See you then."

She replaced the earpiece on its cradle and sighed, flopping back against the pillows.

She had been driving for two straight days, stopping only for sleep and while she had initially thought it would be a depressing trip, Rachel found herself enjoying the time to herself.

How long has it been since I've been embraced by silence? She wondered. She had a hard time recalling the last time.

A fleeting thought of childhood slipped through her mind but she missed it before she could catch it.

She had the dream again, where she was standing in the field, in the snow with someone calling her name.

It was one she had experienced many times over the years but Rachel had never been able to make sense of it.

Forget about the dream, she told herself. *Forget about everything. Turn off your brain and watch television. How long has it been since you've been able to do that without feeling guilt?*

The idea was appealing and she reached for the remote control, flipping idly through the channels. She settled on a light-hearted sitcom but she was asleep before it ended twenty minutes later as if she inherently sensed that the next day would require all her strength.

That night, she did not dream.

"Hey ya! Hey ya!" she scream-sang at the top of her lungs, coasting down Interstate 80. The radio blasted the song but it could not drown out the terrible singing coming from Rachel's vocal chords.

The window was down, despite the freeze in the February day but to Rachel, it was exhilarating.

Wow! She thought. *How long has it been since I've done this? I feel so free, so...unencumbered by everything right now.*

A pessimistic side of her asked how long the euphoria would last.

She decided not to question it, turning up the radio to block out her own dark thoughts.

It was then she heard the thud.

Her heart stopped and instinctively, she slowed the car, looking in the sideview mirrors.

Oh God! Did I just hit something?

She saw nothing, turning off the stereo and steering the vehicle to the side of the road. No sooner did the wheels touch the shoulder did another loud clunk ensue and the car lost power.

Her heart pounding, Rachel leapt from the driver's seat and ran up the shoulder to ensure she had not run anything over.

Relieved that nothing seemed harmed by the U-Haul, she hurried back, rubbing her hands together as the chill crept into her collar.

Well there's my answer, she thought wryly. *It was a short-lived sense of happiness but it was there.*

She crawled back into the driver's side and tried to turn over the engine but it only sputtered, coughing in protest as she attempted.

Great. Now what?

She realized she was in the middle of nowhere, rural Ohio and she silently prayed that she would get reception on her phone.

To her relief, she had weak service and she dialed the operator for help.

Not even going to try for data up here, she thought. To her chagrin, the phone would not dial out.

"Oh come on!" she groaned, jumping from the cab again. She wandered up and down the side of the road, trying over and over as she moved but she got no luck.

Soon enough, however, she saw a car driving toward her and she flagged it down.

The grey sedan slowed and the driver rolled down the window. Rachel ran toward him gratefully.

"Thanks for stopping," she breathed but as she approached, she realized that there was an Amish man in the passenger seat and a lumberjack looking fellow at the wheel.

"You all right, lady?" the driver asked, shooting his companion a strange look.

"My truck just died on me," she said. "I'm heading to New York State and I don't know this area at all. My phone has no reception."

"Yeah, this part of the interstate can be moody with the cell towers," the driver replied. "We can take you to Olena if you want. There's a garage there. Frank can help you out."

Uncertainly, Rachel eyed the unlikely pair.

"Maybe I'll just wait out here," she said, gnawing on her lower lip. "Could you let them know I'm out here?"

The man at the wheel grunted in exasperation.

"Lady, if you ain't got heat, you're gonna freeze. Just get in the car."

Perhaps Rachel had been living in the city too long but she was instantly put off by the man's tone.

"Never mind," she replied flatly. "Sorry to have bothered you."

"Miss, we are going to Olena anyway," the Amish man said quietly and for some reason, Rachel was instantly placated by the sound of his voice. "I would not feel right leaving you here alone. It is dangerous for a woman by herself."

Rachel stared at him, noting his kind green eyes and stoic nature.

She glanced back at her truck, wondering if her belongings would be safe.

You really are becoming jaded, she chided herself. *There are no highwaymen running amok in Amish country.*

"Okay, yes," she decided quickly, sensing the driver's annoyance. "I just have to grab my purse."

She hurried back to the truck and locked up, securing her keys in the depth of her purse before climbing into the back of the car with the strangers.

This is what Dateline episodes are made of, she thought, perching nervously at the edge of the seat as she stared out the window.

"What's your name?" the driver asked.

"Rachel."

"I'm Dave. This here is Samuel. We're from Millersburg."

"Nice to meet you both," Rachel told them, studying their faces. Dave was rough around the edges without a doubt, a burly man who screamed blue collar.

He just comes across as surly but I bet he's a big pussycat, she thought, turning her attention to his quiet companion.

I wonder what they are doing together?

"Where are you coming from?"

"San Francisco."

Dave let out a low whistle.

"That's a long drive for one person. What happened? Got sick of the city life?"

If only, she thought ruefully.

"Something like that." She realized how short her answers had sounded and she instantly felt ashamed.

"I'm originally from New York. My parents are still there," she added, trying to sound friendly. She could not help that her guard was still up.

Dave looked at her through the rear-view mirror and nodded.

"It's a strange route you're taking to get back to New York," he commented and Rachel cocked her head to the side.

"Is it? I swear this is the route my GPS gave. It's the first time I've driven it."

Dave gave Samuel another look which Rachel could not decipher and she felt a strange chill flow through her.

What am I missing here?

She sat back, peering into the snowy landscape and her breath caught suddenly.

It was as if she was back in her dream, staring at the same fields, spinning in circles looking for the person calling out to her.

"We're just getting into Olena," Dave called to her after a few moments. "Bentz's Auto is not far. I hope he can tow your truck. He may need help with that."

Rachel had not thought about that but she was thankful when they pulled up to the garage. Rachel climbed out of the car and paused at the passenger window which Samuel rolled down.

"Can I offer you some gas money?" she asked and Dave snorted.

"Ask Samuel," he replied chuckling and Rachel was confused but she did.

"Samuel? Can I give you some money for your troubles?"

"No," he said softly. "I wish you the best of luck with your journey."

She stared into his vivid eyes and felt as if his words meant more than she could hear.

Rachel nodded, stepping back from the car.

"Thank you. I can't tell you how much I appreciate you stopping for me."

"Be well, little lady!" Dave hollered, pulling away from the garage and Rachel watched them drive away, a strange longing in her chest.

What a strange encounter, she thought, turning back to the small white structure at her back.

She could not shake the feeling that it had meant something.

Rachel grimaced slightly, pacing around the front of the garage.

"No, mom, it's fine," she grumbled. "I don't need dad to drive here and meet me. It's just not going to be towed until tomorrow and...I told you, I'm in Olena, Ohio."

She rolled her eyes heavenward in silent plea.

"I will let you know what the mechanic says but everything is fine. I'm safe and...yes, mom, I promise – "

Her blue eyes darted upward as a familiar car pulled into the small front lot.

"I have to go, mom. Love you."

She hung up the call and stared curiously as Dave pulled the car along side of her.

Samuel rolled down the passenger side window.

"Hello," she said, curiosity lacing her words. "What are you doing here?"

"We wanted to ensure that you were all right," the Amish man said and Rachel found herself inordinately pleased.

"I won't know until tomorrow," she replied. "Dave was right; Frank the mechanic says he can't tow something that size and he can't get a flatbed until the morning."

"What will you do?" Dave called. Rachel had been asking herself the same question. She simply did not have the money to spend another night or two in a hotel but what other choice did she have?

"I – I guess I'm staying at a hotel," she sighed. "Any recommendations?"

There was a short silence and the men looked at one another.

Samuel cleared his throat.

"I have a farmhouse with many rooms," he told her quietly. "You are welcome to stay there free of charge."

Rachel blinked, stunned by the offer.

Is this generosity or something else? She wondered and guilt immediately flooded her. *Really, Rachel, you have spent far too much time in the city.*

As if reading her thoughts, Samuel continued quickly.

"I live there with my two sisters."

Rachel offered him a quick smile.

"That is very kind but are you sure I won't upset the community?"

The question was sincere but Dave howled.

"That depends; are you going to host any wild parties tonight, lady?" Dave chuckled and Rachel looked mortified. "Run moonshine? Host a poker game?"

"No of course not!" she replied indignantly but she saw that Samuel had an amused grin on his face.

"Come on, Rachel. I'm supposed to be picking someone else up in an hour."

Rachel nodded slowly, once more climbing into the back of the car, slightly overwhelmed by the strangers who had appeared seemingly from nowhere.

This time as they pulled away, Rachel instigated the conversation with the men, determined to express her appreciation.

"I think I have lived in the big city for too long," she confessed. "I had forgotten how kind folks can be in small towns."

"You get your good and bad everywhere you go," Dave replied. "Isn't that right, Samuel?"

"Yes," he agreed. "People live by their own moral code. We are all born with a sense of right and wrong. Whether we choose to adhere to it is on us."

Instantly, Dr. Levin's face popped into Rachel's mind and she was filled with bitterness.

No. He stays in San Fran where you left him. Don't let that affect this moment in your life, she warned herself. She returned her focus to her new companions.

"I imagine that you don't have much of a problem in your community," Rachel piped up. Dave laughed again and Rachel felt her cheeks turn pink.

"I'm sorry if I sound ignorant," she said quickly. "I don't know very much about Amish culture."

"I am happy to answer any questions. I am very proud of our heritage," Samuel replied easily and Rachel was grateful for his indulgence. "It is not ignorance if you are willing to learn. And to answer your question, yes, we have those who stray in our community also. God does send temptation forth to test us."

Rachel was once more filled with the sense that his words had an underlying meaning.

Am I a test for him from God?

"Your knowledge comes from living among the Amish, Dave?" Rachel asked. She cringed at her inquiries. They sounded so strange to her own ears.

"I drive for the district. The Amish do not drive themselves so I am essentially a taxi service."

Rachel paled slightly as she remembered Dave's words earlier when she had offered them money.

Why on earth would Dave stop for me on Samuel's dime? That's rude.

"I hope you're not charging him extra because you chose to stop for me," Rachel chuckled, only half-joking as she eyed Samuel.

Dave laughed his boisterous laugh again.

"I should charge him double!" Dave chortled. "I didn't want to stop at all. He insisted that we not only stop but go back and make sure you were okay. I told him you're a city girl. You'll be fine but he was worried about you."

Rachel stared at Samuel, her mouth slightly agape but he turned to look out the window, purposely avoiding her gaze.

Feeling slightly dazed, Rachel sat back.

Did God send me a guardian angel in the form of Samuel? She wondered. It certainly seemed that way.

They arrived at Samuel's farm slightly after five o'clock and Samuel nodded to Dave.

"*Danke.* Will you stop by tomorrow for Rachel?"

"I'll come around noon but I'll give Frank a ring at the shop before I head over this way. No sense in dragging her back to town if the car isn't going to be ready," Dave replied. "I'll only end up bringing her back and I'm sure she's already seen enough of me for a lifetime."

He grinned to show he was kidding.

"Would you call for me?" Rachel asked, still amazed at the good will of the men. Dave gave her a puzzled look.

"Of course, lady. We watch out for each other in these parts."

He smiled then and Rachel was sure she had never seen a lovelier smile in her life. It instantly lifted her spirits and she returned it easily.

"Thank you, Dave," she whispered, raising a hand as he nodded and drove away from the front of the house.

Alone, Rachel looked shyly at Samuel.

"This is all yours?" she asked, gesturing around the vast property. The house itself was elegant but simple and well maintained.

"Mine and my sisters, yes," he replied, extending an arm in gesture for her to approach. "Our parents left it to us when they died."

Rachel felt a stab of sadness.

"I'm sorry," she breathed as they climbed the steps to the front door. "I didn't mean to – "

Abruptly the front door flew open, startling Rachel and two young women stood beyond the screen, staring open mouthed at her.

They were both younger than Samuel, closer to Rachel's age.

"Ah, you are home," Samuel said, pulling on the exterior door. "I hope you made enough supper for a fourth. This is Rachel..."

He peered at her and Rachel cleared her nervousness from her throat, smiling quickly.

"Rachel King," she said, extending her hand toward the awe-struck girls. The took her hand, trying not to stare at her but Rachel could read the excitement in their faces.

I guess Samuel doesn't bring strange outsiders home every day, she thought wryly.

"These are my sisters, Ruth and Miriam Roth."

"Nice to meet you both," Rachel said, stepping inside the house but she had to squeeze past them.

"Welcome Rachel," Miriam said, finally recovering from her shock. "Yes, of course there is always enough food for visitors."

"Rachel will be spending the night. Please ensure there are fresh linens on the bed in the downstairs room," Samuel told them as he pulled off his boots.

Again, the sisters seemed dumbfounded but the nodded, trying to hide their emotions, ducking out of the foyer.

"Samuel, if this is a problem, I can certainly make other arrangements for the night," Rachel told him quickly. Samuel chuckled lightly and removed his hat, running his hand through his dark blonde hair.

"I assure you, it is not a problem. We have a toilet near the kitchen if you should need to wash." He pointed her in the direction and Rachel accepted the cue to go.

She entered the room where a candle was flickering, casting soft shadows along the dark wood trim and Rachel was sure she had never felt more at ease in a bathroom.

It feels like home, she thought and her brow furrowed at the idea.

How could a remote farmhouse in Amish country possibly feel like home?

She splashed cold water on her face and stared at her meteoric reflection in the mirror, she had a spark of de ja vu.

What is it about today? She asked herself. *It's like there's something in the air, something...spiritual or otherworldly.*

There was a tentative knock on the door.

"Rachel? Dinner is on the table."

She was not sure which sister it was but Rachel thanked her and dried her face and hands quickly, moving to join the Roth family.

"Please, sit," Samuel said, smiling. She slipped into a chair beside Miriam as Ruth brought the rest of the meal to the table.

"We pray before we eat, Rachel," Samuel explained. "You are not required to do so if you do not wish."

Rachel stared at them, wide eyed.

How long has it been since I've prayed? She wondered.

"I would like to join you," she told them sincerely. The sisters exchanged a small smile and lowered their heads as Samuel led grace.

As he spoke, Rachel found herself staring up at him, following the words from his lips. A true calm washed through her body.

The siblings raised their heads and began to pass around the platters of food, starting with Rachel's.

"Where are you from, Rachel?" Ruth asked politely.

"I was born in New York State but I have been living in San Francisco," she explained. "I am just on my way home to my family. My truck broke down and your brother was kind enough to offer his assistance."

A look of genuine understanding flowed through both girls as the mystery of her arrival was solved.

"Ah, what a shame," Miriam said. "Does the mechanic know what is the problem?"

"Unfortunately he can't even look at it until tomorrow."

The women made a commiserating noise in unison and Rachel was beginning to wonder if they were twins.

She looked up and met Samuel's eyes. They were bright with amusement.

"King, you say? Rachel King?" Ruth piped up suddenly and Rachel nodded. She cocked her head to the side and studied Rachel's face closely.

"Do you have any Amish roots?"

Rachel almost choked on her potatoes.

She sputtered and shook her head, reaching for some water.

"Pardon me!" she said as she caught her breath. "That went down wrong."

Samuel laughed aloud.

"I think that is Rachel's way of saying she has no ties to the Amish community, Ruthie."

But Ruth did not smile. She continued to stare at Rachel.

"No, Samuel, she's the very image of – "

"Ruth, that's enough!"

Samuel's tone startled everyone at the table equally and an uncomfortable silence ensued. Miriam jumped in to fill the void.

"What do you do, Rachel? Are you a student?"

"I am a nurse," she replied automatically. The table dropped their forks simultaneously, their mouths agape.

I should have said I was a nurse but no need to bore them with the details of my pathetic life right now.

A slow appreciation filled Samuel's eyes.

"You are a healer," he said softly. "That is very fitting."

A warm glow filled Rachel's heart and she lowered her head in embarrassment.

It seemed that every word he spoke to her made her feel light headed.

This is crazy! You can't become smitten with an Amish man you've known for an hour.

But reason didn't seem to help.

Samuel Roth had a strange hold over her, something inexplicable and Rachel was basking in the sweetness of the feeling.

Ruth set her up in the back bedroom on the main floor. It had its own fireplace and the logs crackled as they entered.

"If you should need anything, my bedroom is at the very top of the stairs."

"I have everything I need," Rachel assured her. "You have been more than kind sharing your home and food with a perfect stranger."

"I don't think you are a stranger, Rachel," Ruth muttered as she turned away.

"What do you mean?" Rachel called out to her, a peculiar feeling touching her gut. Ruth paused in the doorway.

"I think you have Amish in your blood."

She was gone before Rachel could question her further, leaving the former nurse to ponder her cryptic words.

Is that why I feel so comfortable here? Do I have Amish ancestors?

It seemed so farfetched and yet...

Weak sunlight spilled into the back room and Rachel woke, surprisingly energetic.

She had slept better than she had in longer than she could recall and she slipped from the bed, determined to make breakfast for the family before they too rose.

It's the least I can do, she thought but as she hurried into the kitchen, she saw she was already too late.

Samuel was at the sink when she entered, his long hair slightly matted from sleep.

"Oh," she said with some disappointment. "I was hoping to be up before you this morning."

He turned, his eyes twinkling.

"That would be very difficult to do," he told her. "I am a farmer after all."

Rachel chuckled.

"Let me help you," she said, stepping toward the sink but he shook his head.

"You are a guest here," he replied. "Please sit. You can keep me company if you wish. Do you drink coffee?"

"I did mention that I was a nurse, right?"

He nodded, his smile widening and Rachel was drawn in by his brilliant white smile.

"Did you ever ask yourself how you came to be here?" Samuel asked suddenly and Rachel's brow furrowed slightly.

Is this an existential question? Probably not.

"Um...well I think U-Haul had a hand in it," she murmured jokingly. Samuel approached her, placing a steaming cup of hot coffee before her.

"You chose and obscure route returning to New York," he told her softly. "Dave and I discussed it at length. There were much better ways for you to have travelled."

Rachel shrugged, unsure of what he was getting at exactly.

"The GPS is not infallible," she replied. "And I have little sense of natural direction."

Samuel began to laugh.

"I think the opposite is true," he replied softly. Rachel sat back and stared at him.

"What is going on?" she demanded. "What are you saying?"

Samuel sat at the kitchen table and stared at her, his green eyes searching her face.

"Do you remember your childhood at all?"

"Of course."

"How old is the youngest you remember?"

Rachel thought.

"Maybe five? Six?"

He nodded.

"Do you ever dream of this place?"

Goosebumps prickled her skin.

"Samuel, you're beginning to scare me," she told him honestly. "What are you talking about?"

"Rachel, you and your family were born here in Holmes County. When you were four, your parents abruptly decided to leave the community and they took you and your little sister with them. No one knows why it happened. There was speculation that your mother was shunned and your father could not live without her."

Rachel stared at him, her jaw almost at the table.

She shook her head.

"No," she protested. "There's no way. My parents haven't even taken us to church."

"Is your sister named Mary? Two years younger than you?"

Rachel felt hot and cold at the same time and she stared at him in disbelief.

It couldn't be and yet...

"How did you know?" she gasped. "How can you remember that?"

Samuel rose and offered his hand to her.

"Come," he said gently. "I want to show you something."

Reluctantly, she followed him to the front door.

They stepped onto the snowy veranda in bare feet and suddenly, Rachel saw it.

It was the field from her dream.

"That was your family's farm," Samuel told her. "You can't see it from here, but the house is slightly over the hill. Our families were neighbors for generations."

The information was overwhelming and Rachel was suddenly weak in the knees. She reached out to grasp a railing but Samuel caught her.

"I have to get out of here," she whispered, her eyes dark with fear. "If we are shunned..."

Samuel shook his head.

"You are not shunned. You have not been baptized. I am certain if you wanted to return, the Bishop could see to it that you are properly prepared for life here."

She stared at him, uncomprehendingly.

"Return?" she echoed. "What makes you think that I want to return here? I don't know anything about your culture."

"It is your culture," he reminded her. "And you make me think you want to return here. You have come here. Something has driven you back here after all these years. Your car has failed you just in the proper place. Something is speaking to you if only you'd listen."

And suddenly every word he spoke made perfect sense.

Everything which has happened has been leading up to this moment; losing my job, leaving California, driving this obscure route.

She looked at him and realized that everything she had ever wanted was in one place and it always had been; she just hadn't known where to look for it.